"I haven't seen *you* since I was eighteen,

but I've been home quite a few times between then and now. I'm a bit hurt you hadn't noticed. I hear you've been busy since you became *the sheriff*."

The boy wilder than the horses her father used to tame had become the man put in charge of policing the entire county.

"Don't worry, you're not the only one surprised by the news," he said. "Though I am impressed at your reaction. Last time we saw each other, you were more on the reserved side."

Remi couldn't help but laugh at that.

"I was a mouse," she exclaimed. "It took college for me to open up."

It was Declan's turn to laugh.

"Being the sheriff has shown me the value of holding your cards close to your chest."

Remi leaned back to mirror his stance.

"Well, it looks like we might have switched personalities since we last saw each other."

Even though she said it, Remi didn't believe it.

LAST STAND SHERIFF

TYLER ANNE SNELL

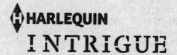

HARLEQUIN
INTRIGUE

This book is for Tyler, my husband. Thank you for always being my smart, hilarious and cat-loving rock. If you're reading this, then let's go make some brownies.

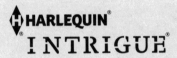

Recycling programs for this product may not exist in your area.

ISBN-13: 978-1-335-13673-2

Last Stand Sheriff

Copyright © 2020 by Tyler Anne Snell

This edition published by arrangement with Harlequin Books S.A.

For questions and comments about the quality of this book, please contact us at CustomerService@Harlequin.com.

Harlequin Enterprises ULC
22 Adelaide St. West, 40th Floor
Toronto, Ontario M5H 4E3, Canada
www.Harlequin.com

Printed in U.S.A.

Tyler Anne Snell genuinely loves all genres of the written word. However, she's realized that she loves books filled with sexual tension and mysteries a little more than the rest. Her stories have a good dose of both. Tyler lives in Alabama with her same-named husband and their mini "lions." When she isn't reading or writing, she's playing video games and working on her blog, *Almost There*. To follow her shenanigans, visit tylerannesnell.com.

Visit the Author Profile page at Harlequin.com.

CAST OF CHARACTERS

Declan Nash—After years of danger surrounding his family, this sheriff is finally ready to solve the coldest case the town has ever had—the Nash triplet abduction. But after a night spent with a woman he's always admired makes him a father-to-be, the stakes only get higher as he needs to keep her out of a conspiracy spanning decades. Will he finally put to bed the ghosts of the past? And can he do it while keeping the mother of his unborn child safe?

Remi Hudson—This former cowgirl left behind the ranch life when she left Overlook years ago. However, after becoming pregnant by her former crush and friend while visiting, she's back in her hometown and in a heap of danger. Can she help the sheriff and his family get the justice they deserve? Or will she be the target that's used to bring them all down?

The Nash Triplets—Known by the town for being abducted when they were eight, Caleb, Madi and Desmond have spent their lives since helping people and trying to move on. But each have faced threats over the last few years that make them wonder if someone hasn't been pulling the strings all along.

Jonah & Josh Hudson— Remi's brothers might be openly disappointed of her life decisions, but when push comes to shove, they'll protect each other at all costs.

Man in the Suit—He's back in town and, if Declan's right, him and his criminal organization known as the Fixers never really left.

Chapter One

Declan Nash wasn't having the greatest of days.

Not only was it raining cats and dogs and elephants, his trusty old pickup had decided not to be so trusty.

"Come on, Fiona." He rubbed the dash trying to coo the truck into stopping her lurching and ominous rattling sound. Fiona the Ford wasn't impressed. Declan admitted defeat by taking the upcoming exit. There was a gas station at the corner of the short road. He pulled in, sighing. "After everything we've been through, you decide to pitch a fit now and here of all places?"

The city of Kilwin, Tennessee, was an hour out from where he had been on the highway. Which meant his hometown of Overlook was an hour and twenty minutes out of reach.

Not that he was reaching for it.

He might have been the sheriff of Wildman County but, as of that morning, he was just a man on vacation.

Or, at least, he was trying to be.

Declan sighed into the empty cab again. His dark blue Stetson, one he only wore on his off days—which meant he hardly ever wore it—sat on the passenger seat mocking him.

"You're about to become an umbrella," he told it.

The rain was having a great old time drenching Declan to the bone after he got out and propped up his hood. He hadn't parked under the gas station awning, worried about his truck catching fire and making a bad situation way worse. That decision got him wet but was reassuring as steam billowed up, angry, at him from next to the engine. There was also an overpowering oil smell.

Declan jogged back to the cab and grabbed his phone.

Just in time for the interior lights to blink out.

His battery had died.

So, Fiona was finally going to pitch a fit. After fifteen years of not making a peep, she was doing it during the first vacation he'd taken in at least five.

Declan hung his head and swore. The motion dumped water from his hat into his seat.

Declan swore some more, spied the diner next to the gas station and decided that he was at least going to get some coffee out of all of this. He could deal with the truck once the rain let up.

Still, he grabbed his duffel bag knowing there wasn't an inch in this world to give when it came to the accordion file he had tucked in with his boxers and toothbrush.

"We'll get you figured out, Fiona," he told his truck with a pat after locking her up. He dashed across the gas station parking lot and right into the diner. When he pushed through the front door, heralded in by a chime, an older woman with a nice smile met him.

"When it rains it pours, huh?" she greeted, motioning to one of the large-pane windows that ran along the front of the building. He could see his truck through the one next to the last booth. "We have some fresh hand towels in the kitchen. I can get you some to dry off a little if you'd like."

Declan took his hat off and pressed it against his chest. He gave the woman—Agnes, according to her name tag—a smile that he meant.

"That would be much appreciated, thank you."

Agnes went off to the kitchen while Declan took the booth in the corner so he could keep an eye on his truck. He set his duffel on the floor next to the seat.

Then he had a moment of internal crisis.

His hands itched to open his bag and pull the folder out, to riffle through the pages he'd already read and reread countless times. To look at every piece of evidence that had been collected for over twenty-five years. To see his own notes and compare them to the ones his father had made when he had been a detective.

Then Declan heard an inner voice warning of doing just that.

It wasn't his conscience; it was a collective featuring Madi, Caleb and Desmond. They'd all made it clear that they were concerned Declan was blurring the line between dedication and obsession. That finding justice, finding the truth, wasn't worth the toll of the quality of his life.

Not after the same obsession had taken their father's life.

Since Declan was their big brother, a part of him prickled at being directed at what to do or, more aptly, what not to do. Just as quickly, though, as his gruffness reared its head, he'd remind himself that in the small town of Overlook, they weren't just bystanders.

Madi, Caleb and Desmond had told him that from experience they knew what it was like to be slowly consumed by a mystery. He had to learn to let go and live a little.

Considering the case was about their abduction, Declan figured they might have a point.

Now, though, with his truck broken down and the rain trapping him inside a diner that had only two other patrons, Declan couldn't help deciding his vacation hadn't *really* started yet. This was more of a pit stop. Which meant if he looked at the files now, it didn't count against him.

Agnes returned with a few hand towels, cutting off the physical action of taking the folder out. He ordered a coffee and some bacon and eggs and returned the towels. Then he retrieved the folder and put it down on the tabletop with minimal guilt and maximum focus.

He hadn't been there at the park that day.

He hadn't been attacked and taken and held in a basement.

He hadn't had to trick a man and fight to get out as the three scared and hurt eight-year-olds had done.

He hadn't had to make the terrifying trek through the woods to find help.

No, Declan hadn't been there at all.

He'd been too consumed with his own little world to notice the triplets had disappeared until an hour after the fact.

And then he'd had to wait with the rest of Overlook for three days, hoping and praying they would find nothing but good news.

Declan could still feel the helplessness that had nearly crushed him during the wait.

And now?

Now Declan was older, smarter.

Now Declan had focus and patience and a lot more experience.

Now Declan was the sheriff.

He couldn't save the triplets from what had happened, but he could damn sure finally give them the peace they deserved.

The rain continued to fall. Music from the kitchen floated to the front. Declan didn't wrestle with his choice anymore. The diner would actually be the perfect place to look over the newer evidence. No one from his family at his shoulder. No one from the sheriff's department by his side.

He opened the folder.

No one was going to distract him here.

The time for questions was over. Now it was time for answers.

REMI WAS, AS her cousin Claudette said, a "Hot Mess Susan."

Not the worst thing she'd been called in her thirty-three years of life but definitely not the most flattering, either.

What was worse than being called a Hot Mess Susan?

When the nickname actually applied to her.

And now, pulling into the diner off Exit 41B, it definitely applied.

Remi cut the engine in a parking spot and let out a sigh that had apparently been trapped in her chest for the last hundred miles. It dragged down her shoulders, slouched her back and put pressure on the stress headache that had been brewing all morning.

"'Go see your father,'" she muttered to no one, adopting her mother's pushy voice. "'It'll be fun. Stop stalling, Remi. It'll be *fine*.'"

Her mother wasn't right about much...and she was wrong about that, too. It hadn't been fine. In fact, it had been awful and exactly what she had expected.

Josh and Jonah had met her with hugs and sibling love, and then all of that mush had soured when their father had sat them down at the dinner table. The questions had started and they'd all daggered her. Remi had felt like she was interviewing for her job at Towne & Associates all over again. However, instead of sitting across from a group of public accountants she was looking at three cowboys who didn't understand a lick of why she'd left the ranch all those years ago in the first place.

Which was why she hadn't told them of her current problem. One that she'd been wrestling with before she ever decided to heed her mother's advice and go see the Hudson men in Overlook.

How she ever thought they'd take a second to think outside of the ranch and help her, she didn't know.

But now with the rain hitting the roof of her car, reminding her that she didn't have a rain jacket or an umbrella, Remi felt her troubles being pulled back to her. That, and the weather, had been one of the reasons she'd taken the exit and parked herself outside of a diner. It's neon open sign was a distraction she was ready to fully embrace.

She grabbed her purse, tucked her phone in the waist of her exercise leggings and tried to think about how see-through her shirt was going to become just from her short jaunt between the car and the front doors.

Then she ran.

And immediately became drenched.

A chime sounded over the door as Remi danced inside. She was met with cool air that made her now-wet clothes cold. A song was playing somewhere in the small space, and through the cook's window behind the counter a man gave her a look. An older woman in uniform also looked through the window and called out.

"Be with you in a sec, hon!"

Remi gave a polite smile and decided not to check her shirt to see if her bra was showing through the beige. Instead, she ran a hand through her dirty-blond hair that was probably dark now and took a quick look at the few patrons already seated.

To her right was a couple immersed in their own conversation, and a gray-haired man in a booth two down from her spot in the middle of the space. Straight ahead was a woman and her small son at the counter, making quick work of what looked like apple pie. To her left sat one man in the last booth.

He was facing her but looking down at the table. Remi noted first that he had wide, muscled shoulders;

second, that he had dark brown hair as messy as hers must be; and, third, that he was, even with his face angled down, attractive. Then, with a little start, Remi realized the fourth and most intriguing detail.

She dripped water across the linoleum and walked right up to a face she hadn't seen in ages.

"Declan Nash?"

The cowboy hat resting on the table was all the confirmation she needed, but the man still raised his eyes to hers and nodded. Remi couldn't help feeling a bit of heat as he looked at her directly.

She saw both the boy her father had warned her about when they were kids and the man who had grown up quite nicely.

When he cut a grin and recognition flared behind his green eyes, Remi felt more heat rising in her.

"Well, if it isn't Remi Hudson."

Declan surprised her by standing and extending his hand. She felt her eyebrow quirk up as she shook his hand.

The young Declan hadn't been so formal, especially when it came to her. Why shake the hand of the person you're competing with or fighting against?

He didn't make a thing about her questioning look as he motioned to the seat opposite him. Before he officially asked her to sit, he looked behind her.

"Are you here alone?"

She didn't miss his glance down at her left hand.

So she held that hand up and thumped her ring finger.

"Alone in the diner and single outside of it."

Declan chuckled as Remi slid across the plastic seat. Her wet leggings made it squeak.

"I don't think I've seen you this close to Overlook since we were, what, nineteen?" He closed the folder on the tabletop and leaned back against his seat. The new position highlighted how the years had been more than kind to the man. His face was all angles and strong. The bump in his nose from the time he broke it after getting into a fight with Cody Callers at a house party when they were sixteen was still visible but, instead of looking awkward as it had then, now it added to the intrigue that was him.

Because, while Remi had known the wild child that was Declan Nash, she hadn't seen him since graduation day.

"I haven't seen *you* since I was eighteen, but I've been home quite a few times between then and now. I'm a bit hurt you haven't noticed. It's not like Hudson Heartland isn't the Nash Family Ranch's next-door neighbor or anything."

"There's a good hundred acres or so between the ranches, so forgive me for not having superhero-grade vision," he teased.

"You're forgiven, I suppose. Besides, I hear you've been busy since you became *the sheriff*."

Saying it out loud created the same shock she'd felt the first time her father had told her about the eldest Nash sibling running for sheriff. When he'd won, well, that had been a much stronger shock.

The boy wilder than the horses her father used to

tame had become the man put in charge of policing the entire county.

"Don't worry, you're not the only one surprised by the news," he said. "Though I am impressed at your reaction. Last time we saw each other you were more on the reserved side."

Remi couldn't help but laugh at that.

"I was a mouse," she exclaimed. "It took college for me to open up and see the virtue of speaking my mind. Something I assume you can relate to."

It was Declan's turn to laugh.

"Being the sheriff has shown me the value of holding your cards close to your chest."

Remi leaned back to mirror his stance.

"Well, it looks like we might have switched personalities since we last saw each other."

Even though she said it, Remi didn't believe it. People couldn't change their stripes. Not when it came to someone as wild and bold as Declan.

The waitress appeared at their table, took Remi's order and was kind enough to give her a hand towel to dab off the excess water. Declan was polite enough to keep his eyes north of her potentially see-through shirt. Sure, he'd been wild when they were younger, but his mama had still raised him right when it came to respecting women.

"So what brings you to this diner?" Remi got around to asking. She looked at the folder beneath his hand. "Is it work related?"

Declan took the folder and slid it beneath his cowboy hat.

"I was actually on my way to one of my deputy's rental cabins for a long weekend." He pointed out the window. The rain had, of course, lessened a minute or two after she'd entered the diner. "You see that—"

"You mean Fiona?" she finished. Like the cowboy hat, Declan had had that truck for years and years. She'd recognize it anywhere and probably would have earlier had it not been raining so hard when she'd pulled up.

Declan smirked.

"Yeah. Fiona." He sighed. "She finally decided to have a fit. I was going to call my roadside assistance when the rain died down since, well, I don't know much about cars."

"Except stealing them from Rodney Becker's garage to prove you were smarter than him," she added.

Declan lowered his voice but there was humor in it.

"Listen here, Huds, you promised you'd take that one to the grave."

The way Declan said the nickname he'd used for her when they were in high school, all rumbling baritone, made some of the heat at seeing him swirl around again. She held up her hands in surrender.

"I keep my promises. But, may I point out, you're not in Overlook right now. In fact, you're not even in Wildman County."

He shrugged.

"You can't be too careful about these things. You know how powerful talk in town can be. One slipup and that's all we'll hear about for years."

He said it in a joking way, but she heard the resentment deep in his words.

Remi was an Overlook native. Her parents had been born and raised in town, and she and her brothers had been born and raised there, too. It was impossible to keep people from talking in a small town, but when it came to the Nashes it was an entirely different ball game.

After what had happened to the triplets, the family had been become famous. A horrible fame that, as far as she knew, hadn't gone away despite the years that had passed.

Remi's coffee showed up at just the right time, and the two of them spent the next half hour talking about the people they'd gone to school with, old friends and annoyances, and what had been going on with their respective families. They hit all the social cues that were expected of a conversation between old acquaintances.

He was sorry to hear about her parents' divorce, and she was happy to hear about his siblings' marriages and kids.

He could barely talk around his laughter about Clay Reynolds being arrested for public intoxication after his girlfriend bought him a fake lottery ticket, and she admitted, with much shame, that she'd dated Matthew Shaker for a year after running into him on campus.

He seemed interested in what her stepfather, Dave, did for a living, and she genuinely was excited that Claire's Café was expanding into the shop next door due to its popularity.

It wasn't until he excused himself to call about Fiona that Remi realized she didn't want the conversation to end just yet.

So when he said that a local mechanic couldn't look at his truck for a few days and would tow it back to Overlook instead, she decided she could take an hour detour back to town.

As long as he'd be with her.

"I don't want to inconvenience you," he said at her offer of driving him back. She waved off his concern.

"You're the one who's going to listen to me talk about my work dilemma all the way there," she said. "May I remind you that I'm an accountant so, honestly, you might just want to ride with the tow truck driver."

Declan smirked.

Hot dog, what a sight.

"I'm always being asked about my job, I'd love to listen to someone else's for a change."

They paid their bill, made arrangements for the tow truck and then headed back to the town they'd both had a mind to leave that morning.

Then the rain went from crummy to bad to worse. It was only when they were between Kilwin and Overlook that they admitted defeat and pulled into another parking lot.

This time it was for a surprisingly nice motel.

"Fun fact," Declan said, pointing in the direction of the vacancy sign. "My sister-in-law is good friends with the woman who owns this place."

"Then I bet you could get us a good deal on a room, huh?"

Remi had meant it as a joke.

Yet, when she looked at Declan, his cowboy hat on

his head and a smirk on his lips, she wasn't quite sure of her own intentions.

She'd always wondered how a kiss between them would feel.

When Declan's eyes moved down to her lips, she had a suspicion he was just as curious.

Chapter Two

A month later and Declan's patience was spread so thin it was damn near transparent.

"Cooper, you called *me* out here, not the other way around," he reminded the always-a-little-left-of-the-law young man. "I have a press conference in a few hours that I need to prep for. I don't have time to just be shooting the breeze."

They were outside the local hardware store, standing in the parking lot between Declan's truck and Cooper's little sports car. Declan was wearing his uniform and had his sheriff's badge hanging on his belt. The black Stetson on his head had just been cleaned. Cooper had on a well-worn Nirvana graphic tee, hole-ridden jeans and an expression that said he needed some prodding to get to talking.

"Come on, Coop," he added. "I'm not a mind reader over here."

The man, twenty-two, cut his eyes to the lot around them and sucked on his teeth a second. Then he got to the point.

"Okay, well, don't get your panties all in a twist, but

I've heard a rumor that I don't think you've heard yet."
He shrugged. "Since you helped me out of that dumb
warrant last year I figured telling you about it would
be a good way to say we're even."

Declan cocked his head to the side, instantly curious. There weren't many rumors that didn't make it to
every pair of ears in Overlook. Considering Cooper
lived in town, Declan couldn't imagine he hadn't already heard it, too.

A day without talk about the Nash family, especially
over everything that had happened in the last few years,
was rare.

"I'm listening."

Cooper stood up straight, no longer leaning against
his car, and dropped his voice a little. Declan couldn't
help but angle forward.

"You know the Waypoint, right?"

Declan nodded. It was a bar in the city of Kilwin,
twenty minutes from Overlook. The clientele had been
mostly law enforcement back in the day. Now it catered
to the crowd in the newly erected business plaza across
the block from it. A family friend who was a detective
with the Kilwin Police Department had said the new
vibe was too modern and trendy for him. Declan hadn't
been there in months.

"Well, for the last month or so there's been a lot of
talk about what happened to your family. You know,
with the, well you know." Declan nodded again. There
was always some kind of talk, even in Kilwin, about
the triplets' abduction, despite it having taken place decades ago. That wasn't anything new.

What Cooper said next was.

"Some guy keeps talking about a note in the wall at the cabin and everyone who knows the story keeps telling him he doesn't know what he's talking about. But he just keeps talking about that darn note in the wall, preaching it like it's gospel. It's probably nothing but I thought I'd let you know."

"A note in the wall," Declan repeated, still not sold.

Cooper shrugged.

"He said it's in the hallway and hidden real good. Said it took the law a while to find it, but I didn't remember hearing that."

There had never been a note found in a wall or otherwise at the cabin where the triplets had been held in the basement apartment. Considering it had been swarmed with law enforcement for months, and revisited by his father for years, Declan was sure he would have known about any note that had been found.

"It sounds like you were listening to a drunk guy wanting attention," Declan said.

Cooper shrugged again.

"Listen, if it had been Piper or that Grant guy who are always trying to rope you into their pyramid schemes, I wouldn't have said anything," he said in defense. "But this guy only ever had one beer in front of him, and it was mostly full. And his suit was so high-end he just kind of seemed to have his crap more together, you know?"

Declan had spent his career in law enforcement learning how to perfect his facial expressions and body language. How to control it so it didn't betray how he was really feeling. In that moment it took all his training to keep his face impassive and his body from visibly tensing.

"That bar has a lot of men in suits, though," Declan said, playing the devil's advocate, careful not to get ahead of himself. "I'm sure more than one of them has their crap together."

"Not like this guy. This dude looked like he belonged on a magazine cover. He looked way out of place there."

Declan's phone started to vibrate. He pulled it out to see a text from his chief deputy, Mayne Cussler. They needed to prep for the press conference.

He sighed.

"I have to get going," he said. Then, with a little more politeness he addressed the young man directly. "Thanks for the info. I do appreciate the effort."

Cooper nodded with a smile.

"Just trying to stay in the sheriff's good graces!"

"I thought you were trying to repay a debt?"

"Can't I do both?"

He laughed and got into his car. Declan, despite the text, hung back as Cooper disappeared down the road.

A note in the wall.

A man in a bar.

A man in a fancy suit.

The last two Declan had run into over the past few years. In fact, a man in a bar had been a detail in the chaos that all three of his siblings had gone through in their personal lives recently.

There had always been a man in a bar who had given bad ideas to bad people.

A man in a fancy suit? They'd run into a few of them, too. Most recently, a man in a high-end suit had gotten tangled up in a dangerous situation with Desmond and his then girlfriend, now wife, Riley. One who actually bore the same scar that the triplets' abductor had had. Though he wasn't the man who had done it, that had been the last new lead they'd had in years.

But a note in the wall of the cabin where they were held?

That was a new one.

And coupled with a man in a suit at a bar?

That was too enticing not to investigate.

Declan put his truck into Drive and moved out onto the road, pointing in the direction that would lead him to that cabin. His phone started to vibrate and he was ready to stall, when he saw the caller ID wasn't one he recognized.

"Nash, here," he answered.

"Hey, Declan, it's me."

That voice gave him a split reaction.

Confusion and primal excitement.

Remi Hudson.

He hadn't seen her since she'd dropped him off at the ranch.

The day *after* they'd stopped at the motel.

"Well, hey there, Huds. How's it going?"

Hesitation, silent and as loud as could be, was his answer. Declan moved the phone away from his face to make sure the call hadn't dropped.

It hadn't.

Remi finally responded.

"I'm, uh, actually in town and was wondering if we could get together?"

She sounded different. Distracted.

It made his gut go on high alert.

"Yeah, sure. I have a press conference in two hours. Can it wait until after then?"

"Oh, yeah, that's fine. Can you just call me back when you're ready? I'll be at my dad's but would prefer to meet up somewhere else."

That didn't surprise Declan. During their last meeting he'd gotten the impression that she was having some issues with her father, Gale, and her brothers. He hadn't pried and he still wouldn't when they met up.

"How about I call you when I'm done and we can meet at my house?"

"Okay, great. Yeah, okay. Well, I guess I'll talk to you later."

Remi ended the call before Declan could say another word.

For the next few minutes he wondered why she sounded so off, but when he turned onto *the* road that eventually led to *the* cabin, all thoughts flew back to the past.

Declan tightened his grip on the steering wheel.

Being haunted by the past was never a good feeling.

REMI FELT LIKE she was about to vibrate out of her skin with nerves. Which wasn't like her at all. Not anymore. Not since she'd grown up.

Yet, there she was, driving up Winding Road toward

the Nash Family Ranch that sat at its end while the butterflies in her stomach hitched a ride for free.

It was only December 10, but it felt like a lifetime had passed since she'd last been here dropping Declan off at his house. She'd been lucky then to avoid his family all while she and the sheriff had been able to avoid talking about what they'd done, *several* times, at the motel. That had been fine by Remi.

She'd always wondered what it was like to kiss Declan outside of a teenage dare and she had found out. Along with a few other exciting things.

Declan hadn't seemed put out in the slightest at their time together, or that it had to end.

They had separate, nonintersecting lives. The only reason they'd run into each other in the first place at the diner had been a fluke. Nothing more, nothing less.

Sure, the entire ride back to her home in Nashville had been filled with thoughts of the man. She'd compared the quiet, reflective Declan to the wild child she'd grown up with. She had tried to recall every piece of gossip about his life since she'd moved away after graduation, and she'd kept thinking about the *move* that had made her see fireworks. Remi would also be lying if she didn't admit thinking about Declan had become a routine thing. Maybe not every second of every day, but occasionally she'd found that her mind had wandered right to a cowboy with a gruff exterior and the softest lips she ever did kiss.

Then *it* had happened.

The heat. And not the good kind of heat. The kind that made her feel sick and worried that she was somehow dying from some rare disease. One second she was *fine* with a capital *F*. The next she was opening her windows and sticking her head out into the cold night air.

When it happened two more times over a few days, Remi had done the only sensible thing.

She'd googled.

Her anxiety had gone through the roof as sicknesses she was *sure* she suffered from filled her computer screen. It just about soared when one answer in particular kept recurring.

That's when she became a mathematician. One who tore through the house looking for her phone and its calendar app. When the numbers didn't match up, she ran them again.

Then she'd given herself a pep talk about the stress of the huge life-changing decision she'd just made.

It was *stress*.

That was it.

That was all.

"Stress my butt," Remi told the inside of her car now as she passed under the ranch's entrance sign with a snort. Remi might have become a woman ready to say what was on her mind, but that didn't mean she was always eloquent about it.

The Nash Family Ranch had several things in common with the Hudson Heartland, and Remi never got tired of admiring both.

The Nashes owned several hundred acres of the most beautiful fields, stretches of forest, natural bodies of water, as well as picturesque farmhouses, barns and a stable. In the distance the rise and fall of mountains could be admired. From Hudson Heartland those mountains were closer. Remi and her brothers had spent many a hiking trip out on them.

The main difference between the ranches was the number of homes on the properties. On their property there were only two. The biggest, a four-thousand-square-foot house was where she'd grown up and where her father and brothers lived now. On the other side of the ranch stood the second home, which belonged to Jerri and Margot Heath. In a role reversal that had been quite the talk of Overlook when it had first happened, Margot was the stable master while her husband kept the main house clean and the useless-with-cooking Hudson brood fed. Their son, around Remi's age, hadn't felt comfortable with the arrangement as he'd gotten older. The moment he'd turned eighteen he'd moved out west.

Not that Remi could fault him for doing almost the same thing she had done.

The Nash family, on the other hand, had several homes across their acreage. According to Declan, not only did he have his own house on the property, but so did Caleb and his wife, Nina, Desmond and his wife, Riley, and his mother, Dorothy, who still lived in the main house. There was even a new set of structures she'd never seen. The Wild Iris Retreat was a nice walk from the stable and run by Dorothy, Nina and Molly, a family friend who also happened to be one of the only friends Remi had kept in touch with once she'd left Overlook.

Remi had been particularly curious about the retreat, considering Madi and her husband, Julian, ran a bed-

and-breakfast on the other side of town but she hadn't pried too much for any more details. Being around Declan had been bad for her focus, especially after they'd done what they had.

It was like eating a slice of the best cake you'd ever tasted and then having to sit next to the rest of it and pretend your mouth wasn't still watering.

A different kind of heat engulfed Remi at the memory. Even hearing Declan's voice over the phone had had an effect on her. She wondered if the feeling was mutual. He'd seemed so surprised by her call that Remi couldn't help but feel a little sting.

As she pulled up to his house, Remi couldn't begin to guess how the news she was about to deliver to the cowboy would be received.

Not only had she taken his advice on her career troubles and decided to accept the job she'd been offered in Colorado, she'd found out two weeks later while packing up her house that she was pregnant.

With Declan's child.

Remi cut her engine in his driveway and jumped out into the cold air. The sound of tires against gravel forced her attention to the truck pulling up behind her from the main road.

Declan gave her a polite smile through the windshield as he parked.

Boy, was she about to blow his mind.

Chapter Three

"Do you mind if we ride out somewhere? I could really use a second set of eyes."

The moment Declan saw Remi outside of her car, he'd had the idea that she could be exactly what he needed. The cabin in the woods was empty, just as it had been for years and years. Declan had swept the hallway before looking through every other part of the space, trying to find a clue he'd somehow missed.

Then he'd left for the press conference.

But his mind was still in that cabin, suspicious of the man in the suit.

When he saw Remi, he realized what he needed was peace of mind. He needed a second pair of eyes, ones that weren't as close to the case as he was.

He needed her to confirm there was nothing there.

Then he could let it go.

For now.

Remi's eyebrow rose in question. She tilted her head to the side a fraction. Her hair shifted at the movement in a sheet across her shoulders. She'd cut it since he'd seen her last.

It looked good.

Then again, Remi always looked good.

"Do I need to wear my good dress?"

Declan didn't understand until she pointed to his suit blazer, pressed button-up, and slacks. He chuckled.

"No. I have to get spiffy for the press conferences," he said. "Something about jeans and flannel not being appropriate."

Remi looked him up and down openly. Declan tried not to do the same.

While he'd in no way expected to do what they had done the day *and night* his truck had broken down outside of town, the truth was they had. And they'd been good at it, too. Just as they'd both been clear about it being a one-time thing.

Two ships passing in the night.

Catching up, and dressing down, with a friend.

Remi had a promotion in wait, he had a county to protect.

She'd left town for one reason; he had stayed for many.

They'd been adults about parting ways. Coolheaded and relaxed.

That didn't mean Declan hadn't occasionally thought he smelled her perfume or snorted at a joke she'd told during their time together.

Remi had been fun to hang out with when they were kids, even when she was quiet. Adult Remi had been a change that he had still enjoyed, as the woman said exactly what was on her mind.

But now, standing opposite her, there was a hesitation that seemed to be moving across her expression. Declan realized he might have done it again. He'd focused on the case more than he had the present. Remi was in front of him, in Overlook, and there he was already trying to rope her into playing junior detective. Why was she here?

Still, it was hard to forget about the note in the wall. It clawed at his mind, despite the company.

"We don't have to go if this can't wait or can't ride along with us?" he ventured.

"Location won't change the conversation," she said with a shrug. "But I am worried you don't remember that I'm an accountant and *not* a detective."

"I need a second opinion, is all."

"And you picked me because you know I have a lot of those?"

She started to walk around him toward the truck. Declan opened the door for her before answering.

"I know you're about the details," he said. Then, moving to the driver's side and sliding in, he gave her an even look. "And I'd like a civilian and non-Nash to help look for those details."

Remi's eyebrow rose again. Declan noted the freckles he'd remembered from her teenage years were still peppered around her eyes and across her cheeks.

"Where exactly are we going?"

Declan put the truck in Reverse. He didn't answer until they were back on the main road that ran through the ranch, heading toward Winding Road.

"The Well Water Cabin."

He could detect her confusion without her voicing

it right away. She shifted, her hair moving across the seat's fabric as she must have turned to look at him. He sighed and explained.

"I heard about a man in a bar who keeps talking about a note in the wall that law enforcement missed. Sounds like a weird riddle or bad nursery rhyme, I know, but I went there earlier and looked around anyways. Like I thought, it was empty. But there are so many coincidences that have popped up lately that I'm inclined to think it might be worth looking into." He gave her a quick look and half shrug. "I also know how close I am to this case and how many times I've been over every single detail. I could be missing something I haven't seen *because* I've seen it too much. You know?"

"Like having someone else proofread an email before you send it off because you've read it too many times already."

Declan snorted.

"Exactly. There could be nothing there and I just can't let go, which I know is a concern. Or, there could be something." He gave her a sidelong glance as they slowed going through the main gate. "I need another set of eyes to proofread."

Remi nodded and stared out the windshield. Her brows were knotted together in thought.

"And asking Caleb, the actual detective, would be worse than going by yourself," she surmised. "Not to mention, he probably doesn't want to go back there in the first place."

"None of them do. Ma won't even drive on the road

that leads up to the place. Not that I blame any of them. They've had their fill for more than a lifetime."

Out of his periphery he saw Remi nod again.

One thing he had valued in his friendship with her when they were younger was her ability to not enjoy the drama surrounding the triplets' abduction. Some people thrived on it, still bringing the case up in casual conversation with throwaway theories about the man behind it. Ones they thought up on their lunch break and brought up like it was some party game. Declan's father had entertained any and all of them, but Declan had had the benefit of seeing his father run himself into the ground and had changed tactics. He and Caleb had heard many theories and kept their expectations at zero.

Still, Declan knew his family wished people would stay quiet about it. He did, too. He and his siblings had spent middle and high school dealing with children and teens with no tact. He'd hoped that as they aged their need to reach into the past and stir up gossip would ebb away.

It hadn't for a majority of Overlook residents.

Yet, Remi had never been one of those people. Whether they were kids or teens, she only spoke on the subject when he brought it up. Even then she stayed thoughtful, not at all interested in fanning the fire.

Now, sitting next to her, Declan was reminded of that thoughtful girl who had been his friend even though she'd adopted a new outgoing personality since college. A part of him wished he'd kept in touch when she left. The other part reminded him that she'd left to get away from Overlook and start a new, different life.

It was for the better.

"What do you mean coincidences?" Remi asked. "People *talking* about the case? Surely that can't be out of the ordinary for around here."

It was Declan's turn to hesitate. The man in the suit. The man in the bar. The man with the scar on his hand. All of that information had been kept within the family and only between the detectives at the sheriff's department and his chief deputy, Cussler. Everyone knew what it meant for any potential new information on the case to get out. What was already a long shot of an investigation would become impossible.

Declan had dropped his guard for one night with Remi, it was true, but they weren't in that room anymore. They weren't in her car, heading home before heading in opposite directions.

What he knew held a weight that he didn't want to put on her even though Declan was taking her back to the scene.

She didn't have to know everything to be helpful, and he decided then and there that he could keep some things from her without being a grade A jackass.

"A few cases have had a similarity that could be connected," he went with. "Again, it might just be someone doing it on purpose to throw us off or pull our legs, but I can't let it go just yet unless I know for sure."

"So, we need to find a note in the wall or nothing at all."

"That's the goal."

Remi smiled. Declan knew because he heard it clearly in her voice. He was surprised at how much he was reminded again of the girl he'd known. Even when she had been quiet, he'd always been able to tell when she was smiling without looking at her.

"Well, I'm sure not about to say no to the sheriff, now am I?"

THE ROAD THAT led to the Well Water Cabin looked like many roads to older houses in Overlook. Dirt mixed with gravel, tree-lined, worn by weather, age and use. Narrow, too. If you met another vehicle you just had to pray you had the good luck that at least one of the two wasn't a truck and that there was enough room to crunch onto the nearly nonexistent shoulder so the other could pass by.

Isolated but not without purpose.

Yet, the road that led to Well Water was different.

It felt almost forgotten. Or maybe lost. Not because of its location and beautiful scenery, nestled within one of the thickest parts of the forest that stretched across Overlook, but because people had tried to lose it.

There was an eeriness that crept into every visitor's bones when driving up to the cabin. Whether they admitted it out loud or not. Remi was sure of that just as the odd feeling moved across her like she'd walked into a cold spot during the summer heat.

While she'd had every intention of telling the man about her pregnancy as soon as she could, he'd said just about the only thing that had made her wait. Or, really, if she was being honest it was the way he'd looked when he talked about going to the cabin. His eyes had somehow softened and remained hard at the same time. Like someone trying their damnedest to appear the picture of strength while trying to hide the vulnerability tearing at them.

It was such an intriguing and surprising juxtaposition that Remi had decided to tell Declan after they had examined the cabin. Maybe the news would cheer him up.

Maybe it wouldn't.

Either way Remi didn't believe there was a note in the cabin, hidden in the wall or not.

Someone would have found it by now.

At least she thought so.

"How did you get in?" she asked as he followed the last curve before the cabin. "Did the Fairhopes give the department a copy of the key?"

The Fairhopes had owned Well Water for years before the abduction. They had lived in Chicago and used the cabin as a vacation home when it struck their fancy. Remi had heard through the grapevine that, after being interviewed and investigated extensively, the family hadn't been back to Overlook. Remi realized she didn't know if anyone else had rented the place from them.

Declan's voice went hard.

"I own it."

Remi's hair slapped her cheeks, she turned her head so fast.

"You own it?"

Declan's jaw was set. He nodded.

"Dad bought it from the Fairhopes. When he passed, it passed on to me."

"That gives me some mixed feelings, I'll be honest."

"You're not the only one."

You'd never guess such a cute, quaint cabin could breed such heartache, confusion and fear.

Well Water came into view like the beautiful terror it was.

Remi had never been inside but, like most of Overlook, had found her way to the outside to look.

A true log cabin exterior with a storybook chimney and wraparound porch. The green on the window trim and front door had aged well over the years, but the front gardens had not. They were equally overgrown and barren.

Declan parked next to the mailbox. Remi watched as he pulled a key out of the middle console. The hardness in his voice had transferred to his body.

She had no doubt he was becoming the sheriff.

There was no banter-heavy lead-up to going inside. No flourish or outpouring of emotion. Declan got out, Remi followed. He unlocked the front door, she moved past him. He hung back by the door, she started to explore. It was a silent dance between them. One that completely consumed her.

As long as they were in *the* cabin, all thoughts of being pregnant with Declan's child, moving to Colorado and how insanely different her life was about to become quieted.

Then it was just the two of them in an empty cabin.

Chapter Four

Well Water wasn't a spacious place by any means. The layout was simple. The front door opened into a narrow hallway that went back to the kitchen but opened up to the living space on the right and two small bedrooms and one bathroom on the left. The stairs to the basement were pushed against the only stretch of wall between the living room and the doorway to the kitchen. Down there, however, things took a turn for the creepy. That was where the Nash triplets had been locked up. A basement apartment was how it had been described in the news. A bedroom, kitchenette and bathroom.

A door that had once had four sets of locks on the outside.

Remi didn't want to go down there yet. Instead, she walked through every room upstairs with fresh attention.

First of all, she was surprised that the cabin was fully furnished. She'd expected to walk into an empty, stale space. Instead, it looked very much like a vacation home, albeit from the eighties. Some furniture was covered with drop cloths, other pieces had a thin layer of dust. Again, she never would have picked this place to be the site of a town-wide legend whose story continued to terrorize.

Remi was careful as she picked her way through each room until eventually she made it back to the hallway.

Declan looked like a statue leaning against the wall opposite the bedroom and bathroom doors. Cast in stone, the man was rigid. Jaw set sharp and intimidating, shoulders broad and unrivaled, muscles a testament to his discipline and focus, and bright green eyes narrowed and seeing only the past. Remi felt a tug at her heartstrings for him. The greatest upset in her family life throughout her existence was her parents' divorce and, honestly, it had been a blessing for everyone. She hadn't had to deal with fear and then death like he had.

And she certainly hadn't taken those experiences and been elected into a job that dealt in both on more than one occasion.

"If there's something here, I'm not seeing it," she said with sympathy. He nodded and tried to smile. It fell short, but Remi wasn't going to fault him for it.

"It's okay. I guess I didn't expect there to be something."

Remi glanced at the stairs across from him.

"So do we go down there next?"

Declan sighed. He took off his Stetson and thumped it against his thigh.

"This place has gotten a lot of attention but downstairs is another story altogether. I'm confident that not even a speck of dirt has gone undocumented from that apartment." His attempt at a smile dissolved completely.

It looked so odd in comparison to the faded but still bright blue paint that covered the hallway's walls. The rest of the rooms were painted in similar, bright shades. Remi had somewhat expected wallpaper given the date of the cabin, but all the other rooms had a texture to them like they'd been sponged instead.

She guessed the Fairhopes hadn't liked the effort since the hall didn't have the same effect. It looked like they'd simply painted over wallpaper. Remi could see the seam right above the wooden chair rail that ran around the hall.

"We can go," Declan continued. "You've already done enough by just coming out here."

He pushed away from the wall, but Remi didn't move. She felt her eyebrows furrow in together as she continued to stare at the wall.

"What is it?" Declan asked. He turned around after Remi pointed.

"That seam that's been painted over."

"You mean the wallpaper? Yeah, they painted over it."

Remi shook her head, finger still poised in midair, and looked around the small hallway.

"Where are the other seams?" she asked. "If you paint over wallpaper you're going to see more than one, or bubbles from the paint over the paper. Something over the chair rail or at the corners. Not just *one* seam. No one is that good at painting over wallpaper, especially not in the eighties or nineties."

Declan touched the seam beneath the paint.

"Unless it's not a seam from wallpaper."

Green eyes met hers. Remi saw the excitement. The potential. The possibility that they were close to something new. She felt it, too.

What she didn't expect was what happened next.

Declan touched the wall next to the seam and then reared his arm back and punched that same spot. Remi gasped as his fist went right through the drywall.

"Declan!"

"I'm okay," he said. Then he did it again, beneath the hole he'd just made. It expanded the open space. Remi was prepared to grab his arm to keep him from doing it again when he slowly put his hand into the hole and pulled more of the drywall out. It came off with ease. He tossed the blue-painted chunks to the left of her. There was no trace of wallpaper on any of the pieces.

Then he kicked the wall, opening a new hole.

Remi took a step back.

It was oddly intriguing to watch the man pull, punch and kick away an entire panel of drywall with such ease. And in a blazer and slacks, no less.

Soon there was a Declan-sized hole in the wall. Remi moved closer again as the sheriff stepped just enough inside of the hole to peer straight at the spot where the seam was. Without looking anywhere else, he pulled two things from two separate pockets of his blazer.

One was a pair of plastic gloves, which he put on with lightning speed and precision. The other was a pocketknife.

He opened it, wordlessly.

Then he slid the blade beneath the seam like an expert surgeon.

Remi held her breath.

The chill from outside had found its way into the cabin. Goose bumps moved across her skin.

A long, agonizing minute crept by.

When it was over Declan had cut out what had made the seam.

"My God," he breathed out after holding it up. He met Remi's gaze with a look of total bewilderment. "Huds, it's a piece of paper."

THE PAPER WAS small but thick. One side was covered in paint, but the blue hadn't bled all the way through. The ink that was scrawled across the other side, the one that had been against the original cream-colored wall, was still legible.

In fact, it was nearly pristine.

"What does it say?"

Remi followed him into the kitchen, careful to keep her distance as he gently laid the paper down on one of the counters. The power was off, but the natural light kept the first floor bright. Still, Declan set the paper beneath the window that ran across the kitchen wall, not wanting to miss a thing.

"It's a name." The handwriting was tight, neat. Declan didn't recognize it, though he did the name. "Justin Redman."

"Who? Is that all it says?" Remi went from a careful distance to right up against his side. She smelled like the beach. Sunscreen and sunshine. It might have knocked him off his game had they been in a different setting.

But not now.

Not here with the note from the wall.

"That's all it says," he confirmed, tilting the paper up so she could see it better. "Justin Redman."

"Does that name mean something to you?"

Declan nodded.

"He was a part of one of the cases my dad was working when the triplets were taken. Aggravated assault. Redman was attacked outside of the old gas station at the turnoff to County Road 11. The one that shut down when we were around fifteen, sixteen. He couldn't give a good description and there were no witnesses. Then Redman died in a car accident. The department never found out who attacked him but suspected it was drug related." Declan pulled out his phone to take pictures. "I don't know why his name would be here. Or, for the matter, why it was painted against the wall."

"Or how that man in the bar knew about it," Remi added.

A shot of adrenaline went through Declan.

"Or how he knew about it," he repeated, chewing the words over.

Remi shifted and walked away. Declan took several pictures before laying the paper gently back down on the cabinet.

"What are you doing?" he called.

"What do you think I'm doing? I'm looking at the walls again! Check for any seams or bubbles or discoloration. If there's one hidden piece of paper, who knows how many more there might be!"

Declan followed his rising excitement and Remi's instructions. Together they inspected the first-floor walls in silence. Sometimes Remi would be the one running her hands over different spots, other times Declan would rub certain stretches of faded paint.

When they ended their search at the top of the stairs again, Declan took pictures of the wall he'd partially demolished.

It had been easy to punch through the drywall but had left his hand stinging. A glance down showed blood. He tried to keep that hand out of Remi's view.

"What now? Do we go downstairs and look?" Declan was surprised at how eager Remi was to help. Surprised and pleased. It helped remind him how easy it had been to hang out with her as kids and teens. Being in her company was nice now, even if they were looking for hidden clues in walls.

It also reminded him how bizarre their current situation was compared to them hanging out in the loft space of his family's barn or out behind the high school complaining about Mrs. Darlene's too-hard geometry homework and Coach Kelly's ridiculous rules about dressing for PE.

Declan was surprised at himself for what he said next.

"We got way more than I bargained for already. I need to take that paper back to the department and do some digging. I can come back out here later and look downstairs, though I stand by there being not a speck of dirt or dust down there that hasn't been cataloged already." He motioned to the walls around him. "This, though… This was a surprise."

"Are you sure you don't want to keep looking? I don't mind."

Declan shook his head.

"You've done more than enough already, Huds. Thank you, I mean it."

Remi's cheeks darkened slightly. From rosy to rosier. She was blushing. It was an endearing sight.

"It was no problem."

Declan went out to his truck, grabbed one of the plastic sandwich bags he always carried in the cab, and bagged the note. Remi waited outside, leaning against the truck and looking off into the woods. It was a nice sight when he came back out, ready to leave.

It wasn't until they were both back in the cab of the truck that Declan realized the weight of what they'd just done.

What they'd found.

A new clue to the abduction case.

The case that had torn his family apart.

The case that changed all of their lives.

Justin Redman. Declan had already reviewed the cases his father had worked on through his career. Michael Nash had been a great detective. Which had been the leading point of fact that had contributed to his obsession with the case and then led to his downfall. He was the great detective who couldn't for the life of him solve an inch of what had happened to his own family, in his own hometown.

It wore him down until there was nothing left.

And now Declan had a piece of something his father had never seen.

Could this be the missing part of the puzzle that finally led to some answers?

Could he finally help his family find the peace they'd been searching for?

A hand touched his arm. Declan was startled by it. Remi's eyebrow was arched, her expression soft.

"Did you say something?"

She smiled. It was soft, too.

"I asked if you were okay."

Declan took off his hat and set it down on the center console. A restlessness was starting to settle on him. An itch he needed to scratch. But that was how it had started with his dad—focusing to the point of isolating himself.

Declan didn't want to do that.

Not to the woman who had seen what he couldn't.

"Sorry," he said, starting the truck. "I get caught in my own head sometimes. Yeah, I'm good."

"And that blood on your hands?"

Declan smirked.

"Hazard of the job."

That earned a snort from Remi, and soon they were back on the dirt road.

The farther away they got away from Well Water, the more he tried to relax and be in the moment.

It wasn't until they were on the main road pointed back to Winding Road that Declan realized how much of a grade A jackass he'd still managed to be.

"What are you doing?" Remi asked the moment he slowed and started to pull onto the grassy shoulder.

Declan switched on his flashers, put the truck in Park, and turned in his seat to face her.

"You called me because you said you wanted to talk, and I pulled you out to a crime scene without even asking what it was that you wanted to talk about. I swear my mama taught me manners. Now what's on your mind?"

A peculiar look changed Remi's expression from confusion to somewhere between amusement and hesitation. He thought she might not tell him for a moment, but then she angled in her seat to face him better and began.

"Well, you know how stressed I was trying to decide if I should take the job in Colorado and you said you thought I should?"

He nodded.

"Yeah! You said it would be a huge step in your career, right?"

It was Remi's turn to nod.

"It would be and, the Monday after I left here last, I accepted the position."

Declan smiled.

"That's great, Huds! You busted your tail to get it!"

Remi's cheeks tinted a darker shade of rosy again.

"It *is* great. I've actually already started packing up the house. What's *not* great is how slow that's been going since the morning sickness kicked in last week."

For a second, Declan thought he heard her wrong. Then Remi raised her eyebrows as if to say, *Yeah, you heard me right, big man.* When she didn't speak for another moment, Declan realized he must have heard her right.

Then he finally added up some things he should have probably already been questioning.

Declan might not have been as good a detective as his father or his brother but, by God, he'd be a damn near a fool to not understand the real reason Remi Hudson had come back to town again.

Chapter Five

"You're pregnant."

It was more a statement than a question, one that didn't seem to match Declan's increasingly inquisitive expression. Remi didn't know what she had hoped to see from the man at the news but was glad, at least, he hadn't tried to rebuff her immediately.

And that she hadn't had to spell it out for him, either.

"According to the lab tech who took my blood and the nurse who called me with the results," she said with a nod. "Not to mention more than a few tests." Remi pulled her phone out and went to the Gallery app. When she got to the cluster of pregnancy test photos she'd taken originally in disbelief, she passed him the phone.

Declan was quiet as he swiped through them. There was another odd contrast between the muscled sheriff and her pink-and-blue-floral phone case. He stopped on the last picture and zoomed in with his fingers, expanding the part of the digital test that clearly read "pregnant."

"You're pregnant," he repeated when he was done. Remi took her phone back. Their fingers touched. Declan was warm. Just as he had been the night that had led them to this moment.

"I didn't notice at first that my period didn't come, and then when I did I assumed it was because of stress, but then I was *just so hot* and Googled my symptoms. I started to do the math. I grabbed a test and made an appointment the next day for the blood draw. Though they took a urine test, too, and it was also positive."

Declan's expression was passing from curious to shocked. His green eyes, tall grass in a breeze, were the size of quarters. A man trying to process as much information as he could while seeking out more.

"But we used protection," he pointed out.

"And yet, here we are at almost six weeks. I guess the Nash swimmers are Olympians."

"Six weeks?" Declan's voice jumped at that.

"Five weeks, five days. Based on conception since, well, that was easy to pin down." Remi held her phone up again. "I have an app that I can show you. It explains *a lot*, which is good because I grew up with three men and—" Before she could finish the thought Declan's cell phone shifted their focus. A rhythmic set of beeps filled the space of the cab around them. Remi could see the caller ID read Detective Santiago. Declan didn't reach for it.

"My news isn't going anywhere," she said with a light laugh. "You can answer the phone. I won't be offended."

Declan still wavered, but by the fourth ring he hit Answer.

"What's up, Jazz?"

A woman's voice floated from the receiver, though Remi couldn't hear what she was saying. A slight panic took over as Remi realized she didn't know if Declan had started seeing someone in the time after they'd been together. She *had* told him several times he needed to lighten up and live a little as they'd been trapped between the sheets together. Had he taken her advice as she'd taken his about her promotion?

And, if so, did it really matter?

Remi did want children. Eventually. Now was unexpected, but she was taking the surprise with a cautious, slightly terrified smile of acceptance. Telling Declan had never been a question in her mind.

However, her expectations of a future together had never been set.

Declan Nash might have been wild when they were younger, but his love for his family had never been in question. He adored his mother, looked up to his father, and he'd die to protect each and every one of his siblings. The man he was now? Remi was seeing the sheriff, a respected man filled with responsibility and the need to protect. Even now, years and years later, he was still trying to protect that same family he'd fiercely loved when they were younger.

No, there was no doubt in Remi's mind that Declan would absolutely step up to his role as father.

What she *didn't* know was what that meant for the two of them in the future.

And where that future might take place.

Because, as much as she liked and respected the man next to her, Remi hadn't for a moment wavered in her desire to move to Colorado. As she'd told Declan when they last spoke, her new job wasn't just a career maker. It paid extremely well.

Financial stability hadn't always been something the Hudson family could claim, and Remi would be damned if she didn't change that for her kid.

She didn't have to hear the conversation going on next to her to read the changes in Declan's demeanor. The shift to sheriff was quick. His brow furrowed, his forehead crinkled, and a frown ate away whatever emotions he was feeling about the news she'd given him.

He nodded even though Detective Santiago couldn't see it.

"Yeah, you were right," he said, gruff. "Thanks for the heads-up. I appreciate it." A sigh pulled his chest down. "Yeah. I'll head that way after I change. Give me twenty."

He ended the call. Then he was staring again.

"I have a *situation* I need to take care of at work."

"Everything okay?"

That sigh came back. She didn't like how it brought the man down.

"Everything is up in the air," he answered. "I'll know more when I get there. Is that okay?"

Remi held her hands up to show no offense was being taken again.

"Listen, I promise you that me being pregnant hopefully isn't going anywhere. We can talk about it more later on. If you want."

Declan's expression was hard.

"I want to."

He put them back on the main road and soon they were on Winding Road, leading up to the ranch. In the time between their stop and the arch that read Nash Family Ranch, Declan had called two people and hurriedly given them information she didn't understand. Remi wasn't trying to snoop, though. Instead, she watched out the window as trees whipped by. Winter had stripped some of them bare. Others were shades of dark green and dark brown. Remi wondered if it would snow for Christmas.

How would the holidays look now?

She started her new job two days into the New Year. This was the last time she'd be in Tennessee for the foreseeable future.

How would her family take the news that she was moving so far away? Not well, she imagined. The last time she'd come to town she'd almost told them about the decision she had to make. To accept the new position or not. Yet, she'd found herself back in their old fights of leaving the ranch for school and after. Moving to Colorado? She doubted that conversation would end in anything but a fight. Especially once she added in the news of a baby on the way.

"Sorry," Declan grumbled as he ended his last call. He cut the engine in the driveway at his house. "If it's not one thing, it's another."

"Well, I'm sure that note and, well, *this*—" Remi motioned to her stomach, which was bloated if she was being honest "—isn't helping your sheriff to-do list."

She meant the comment in humor; Declan didn't smile.

"How long are you in town for?"

"Until Christmas, though I might head back if I need a break from the boys at the ranch."

"Have you told them yet? About, you know?"

Remi let out a sigh that mimicked Declan's earlier stress-infused ones.

"No. Other than the nurse and lab tech, you're the only one I've told so far." She gave him a look she hoped was severe. "And I'd like to keep it on the down low for now. Not only is it too early to tell anyone, I also feel like *we* need to talk it out first."

"Agreed. What about tonight?" He nodded out the windshield. "I can make us dinner. If you don't mind subpar cooking."

Remi couldn't help laughing.

"Considering the microwave was my most-used appliance at my rental in Nashville, anything you make I bet would be ten times better than what I would cobble together at Heartland."

After they got out of the truck, Declan paused next to her car door. He looked like he wanted to say something and couldn't seem to find the right words. Remi felt a wave of sympathy wash over her. In its wake was a surprising and vicious pull of the fear of the unknown.

She could have misjudged the man opposite her. Children and teens *did* grow up, and there was no denying he had. He could still love his family. That didn't mean he would want to be a part of their child's life.

Either way, Remi wasn't about to find the answer right now. She put her hand out and patted Declan on the shoulder.

"Let me know when you want me to come over and I'll be here," she said, trying to sound happier than her thoughts had just become. "And try not to stress too much about everything. I can already see some wrinkles trying to break through."

He smiled. It was tight.

"I guess you're too short to see some of the gray hairs I've been sprouting already."

"Just remember, that's when cowboy hats serve a dual purpose. Slap that puppy on and aim that stress somewhere else. Okay?"

He nodded, but she knew her words were just words. They didn't have the power to wring the stress from his life. Just as his didn't have the power to smooth over hers.

He opened her car door and shut it gently when Remi was inside. By the time she was pulling out of the driveway, she couldn't help but look in her rearview.

Declan was already gone.

COOPER MANN LOOKED two shades of panicked when Declan walked into the viewing room at the sheriff's department. The young rebel was handcuffed to the metal table in the room opposite, visibly freaking out even though there was a thick, soundproofed two-way mirror between them.

Detective Jazz Santiago, Caleb's partner and best friend, shook her head in greeting.

"I couldn't believe the call when it came in," she started. "I almost asked if there was another Cooper

Mann who drove a white Corvette with a piece of duct tape along the bumper."

"But there's not," he finished.

She shook her head.

"Still hard to believe, though."

Declan had to agree with her there.

"Where's the woman he tried to grab? You said her name was Lydia?"

Jazz pulled a slip of paper out of her pants pocket. She handed it over. "Lydia Cartwright" was written in sloppy handwriting. It was a far cry from the neatness of the note he'd found less than two hours ago.

If the current situation hadn't been what it was, Declan would have considered telling Jazz what he had found. Even though she and her husband had lived in Overlook for years, they weren't locals. Her fascination with the triplet abduction stopped and started only when it was relevant to the conversation and only if that conversation was started by a Nash. Her loyalty, friendship and top-notch detective skills would be an asset to figuring out whatever it was that Declan and Remi had found.

Yet, he held his tongue and forced himself to focus on the present and the woman who had almost been kidnapped herself.

"She's at the hospital getting seen about still," Jazz answered. Her shoulders tensed. "He cut up her face pretty good with the keys on his key ring. You can still see some of her blood on his hands."

Declan cursed beneath his breath. Sure enough he

could make out smears across parts of Cooper's hands and fingers.

"Is Caleb out there with her already?"

Caleb had been one of his calls as Declan tried to assess the situation before knowing all of the facts. He'd needed to deploy one of his best to figure out those facts. Pronto. But then he'd spent the majority of the ride over talking to his chief deputy. Mayne Cussler was, and had been, Declan's right-hand man for a while now. When Declan had nearly died a few years ago, Cussler had stepped up in a big way while making it known he liked where he was.

"Being sheriff one day could be nice," he'd said once Declan had been cleared for work again. "But I like where I am right now."

Cussler was a reserved man, quiet. He hadn't been as much when Declan had told him that Cooper Mann had tried to abduct a woman. In fact, Declan had heard the man cuss more during their conversation on the drive over than Declan had heard in the ten years of knowing him.

"Yeah. He and Nina were downtown with Parker when you called so he was able to get there pretty quick," Jazz answered. "He said he'd update us the second he finds something out."

Declan nodded. He tried to untangle the knots of facts threaded together in his head. One line of thought was begging to be pulled out, but Jazz angled her body toward him and dropped her voice before he could inspect it.

"Cooper isn't asking for a lawyer. He's asking for you. He said you two met up today?"

The question of "why" was clear in her expression, yet he was glad there was no suspicion there. She might not have been Declan's partner but she trusted him.

Which made his omission of the entire truth even harder to tell her.

"He heard a rumor about the triplets' abduction case and wanted to pass it on to me, to pay me back for helping clear his warrant."

Jazz's eyes widened considerably.

"What was the rumor?"

That one thread of thought, begging to be pulled out, became the only one left in his head.

"It doesn't matter," he said, anger rising. "I have a feeling it was all just a distraction."

The paper in the plastic bag in Declan's pocket felt heavier. The hope Declan had been harboring since Remi had pointed out the seam in the hallway was now souring into him feeling like an idiot.

Cooper Mann had, for whatever reason, set him up.

He should have known better.

And that just made Declan angrier.

"It's time for me to have a little talk with our friend."

Chapter Six

Cooper was sweating bullets. His face had paled considerably from earlier that morning. There was a slight shake to him. He wasn't exactly the picture of a man who had brazenly attacked and then tried to kidnap a woman. But Declan was no stranger to the adage that looks could be deceiving.

He settled into the metal chair opposite Cooper in the interrogation room and laced his fingers over the top of the table, leaning in. Declan was outraged and trying his best not to let it show.

Cooper, again, wasn't faring well when it came to keeping his own emotions in check. Declan didn't get a word in before the young man was nearly talking over himself to get his side of the story out.

"I didn't do this, man, you gotta know that, right? She came after *me*!"

"Don't call me 'man,'" Declan responded, voice even. "It's Sheriff Nash."

Cooper's eyes widened, a deer caught in headlights. He shook his head.

"*She* came at *me*, Sheriff Nash," he tried again.

"Honest to God, I was just stopping to get something to eat, and she got my attention and then *bam*!" He tried to bring his hands up to his face. The handcuffs kept the movement from extending past his chest, so he jerked his head down to meet his hands. He didn't touch his face but made stabbing motions. "She grabbed my keys out of my hand and started shredding her own face!"

If Caleb had been sitting next to him, Declan imagined he would have snorted and said something along the lines of *Well, that's a new one*.

However, Declan wasn't in the mood in the slightest. He wasn't about to encourage Cooper's story.

"The man who called 911 said he came out of the shop because he heard her screaming and saw *you* trying to push *her* into your car."

Cooper made a strangled sound between frustration and fear. He hit his hands against the top of the table.

"I was trying to get her *out* of my car! After she did that crazy thing to her face, she opened my door and tried to get in! I thought she was trying to carjack me! Then someone was grabbing me and you guys showed up acting like I was the bad guy!"

Declan didn't roll his eyes.

He wanted to, though.

"Why would she want to do all of that?" he asked.

"The hell if I know! She's crazy!"

Cooper was nearly panting. Declan believed something traumatic had happened. What he was having a hard time believing was that Cooper had been the victim.

"You have to understand how this looks from my

point of view, Cooper," Declan said, easy on the tone. "First you come to me today about new information on the abduction case and then you're seen with an injured woman who swears you tried to abduct *her*. Were you trying to use the triplets' abduction to distract me from you trying the same? Or were you just trying to double your chances at making headline news?"

Cooper opened and closed his mouth a few times. Objectively, Declan thought the boy looked terrified and surprised at the accusation. Then again, trying to abduct someone on his watch wasn't just an affront to Declan's job, it was a hard prod into his family's past.

He wasn't going to give Cooper an inch.

Not until he had proof otherwise.

"After we finish talking to Ms. Cartwright, I'll be back in here," Declan said, standing to his full height and drawing in his chest with authority and sincerity. He adjusted his Stetson and made sure his sheriff's badge was showing. "Then we're going to get to the bottom of this. And, Cooper? If you lie to me, you're going pay for that lie. It's as simple as that. Got it?"

This time Cooper found his words. They jumbled together as he again tried to tell Declan he was innocent, that Lydia had been the one lying, and he'd just been in the wrong place at the wrong time.

Declan shut the door behind him with Cooper still talking.

Jazz met him in the hallway.

"This is going to be a nightmare in the press," she said. "Cussler can only sweet-talk Delores and the media away for so long."

"I know." Declan sighed. "Which is why we have to move fast and get this thing settled before it takes over the town."

DECLAN DIDN'T CALL.

Remi shrugged deeper into her jacket and kept her leisurely pace along the dirt path across Hudson Heartland. It went from the front door of the house all the way to the front gate, and she was on her way back for the second pass. The distance wasn't anything she couldn't handle, yet she felt a soreness already creeping into her legs. She was also somewhat out of breath.

Was that a pregnancy thing?

Or was she just looking for pregnancy symptoms and finding her own when there were none?

Remi shook her head. She needed to calm down. Her next appointment was at eight weeks, a little too far away if she was being honest, and she'd given herself that deadline to figure out what the heck was going to happen next for her, her child and Declan.

She knew the sheriff was out there being the sheriff, yet, when seven o'clock turned into eight and then nine, Remi had felt a sting of rejection at his absence. Rescheduling their talk was okay—she'd understand that—but Declan hadn't even texted her.

The reasons he hadn't gotten in touch with her all stemmed from issues Remi had been afraid of when she found out about the pregnancy.

Declan being so busy with work that he'd forgotten about their chat was the leading suspect in her mind. Which opened up a Pandora's box of potential issues for her. One, Declan's job was chaotic and dangerous. Not a point against him but definitely not a point of stability for Remi's comfort or liking. Two, he was a sheriff who didn't just do his job, he *was* his job.

She took in a deep, cooling breath. She'd recognized the look in Declan's eyes after finding the note. It was one of purpose. It was one of excitement. It was a solid stubbornness.

Stubbornness to do whatever it took to see through what he meant to see through.

She'd encountered it before in her father. A dogged approach to life: the job came first because it had to, the rest of them be damned.

Remi knew the balance between family and obligation to protect that family was a difficult dance. One her father had lost when she was younger, resulting in her parents' divorce. And that had revolved around taming horses for clients and then boarding horses, not solving kidnapping cases and trying to protect an entire county of people.

She also knew that she and Declan were friends who had *momentarily* become more.

Could she really expect him to keep her within his orbit? Especially with his job?

And if Declan *hadn't* forgotten about her?

Well, then, that was another set of issues she'd have to deal with.

Remi saw movement ahead of her. The outline of a man was illuminated by the exterior lights set up around the house. For a moment her stomach turned into an excited mess of static, then she realized the proportions of the man didn't fit the wide stature of the sheriff.

He came close enough that the light shifted. Jonah had his eyebrow raised in question.

"You know it's cold out here, right?" he greeted, zipping up the plaid monstrosity their mother had given him a few Christmases ago. Of all the Hudson clan, Jonah and Remi resembled each other the most. Lean, on the shorter side, dark blond hair, and freckles that had faded since they were children. Along with their mother, they both had almond-brown eyes. Remi had liked to think hers resembled more of a burning ember in the right light, but she seriously doubted Jonah would ever want such a frilly descriptor of his features.

Jonah Hudson might have looked like her, but he was all their father in personality. No-nonsense, no-frills, just hard work and a stifling need to guilt others about family obligation while rising to equally intense and set-way-too-high family expectations. Jonah might have been a year younger than her but Remi had always felt he was light-years older.

Even now his gaze felt belittling.

It did nothing for her current mood.

"You know that's what jackets are made for, right?" She motioned to hers and returned his eyebrow raise.

Jonah rolled his eyes but turned so he was at her shoulder. He matched her steps as she followed the curve of the path that went around the house and to the back porch.

"I don't know why you're out here right now anyways," Jonah kept on. "Last I heard you weren't a fan of the ranch. Now you show up two weeks early for the holidays and you're out walking it?"

Remi groaned.

"Just because I don't want to run the ranch doesn't mean I can't love it, you know," she shot back, neck getting hot as her anger spiked.

Jonah raised his hands in surrender.

"I didn't come out here to fight," he backtracked. "I saw you and thought I'd join you. Dad and Josh are in a mood together."

Remi heard the annoyance she often felt for the three Hudson men coming out of one of those men now. Her anger took a turn for the curious.

"Really? I didn't pick up on that at supper."

Jonah's breath misted out in front of him for the smallest of seconds. It wasn't cold enough to sustain a more noticeable cloud. It *did* show Remi a frustrated side of her brother that wasn't, for once, aimed at her.

"You haven't exactly been around the last few years so that doesn't surprise me. Dad and Josh butt heads more and more every day, but ever since Josh started dating this new woman he's been more *vocal* than normal. One moment he's talking about turning the ranch back into *the* place to tame and train horses, the next he's talking about running off into the sunset with this new fling."

Remi was absolutely stunned at that news. A common theme she'd encountered since leaving for college had been how living a life outside of the ranch was akin to familial treason. Josh hadn't pulled any punches as Remi had decided to commit that treason with every new choice that wasn't coming back to Overlook and taking an interest in Hudson Heartland.

"A fling is making him rethink his gospel?" Remi mocked, unable to keep the bad feelings of her brother's disappointment from slinking into her words. "Does that mean I finally get a pass if he decides to run off into the sunset?"

"This is serious, Remi," Jonah tried. "He barely knows this woman and yet he's ready to throw everything he's worked for away? For what? A few rounds in the sack?"

Remi made a disgusted noise.

"I don't need to hear that," she said. "Please and thank you."

They made it to the back porch. The light in their father's bedroom room was off. Josh's room was at the other corner of the house along the back. His light was on. Jonah looked up at it with concern clear on his face.

Despite their differences and the chasm that had opened up between them since becoming adults, Remi softened and took pity on her little brother.

"Josh will be fine. He's been the dutiful son, brother and horse trainer since he could walk and talk. Let him have his moment. If you don't, you'll only be pushing him to do the exact thing you don't want him to in the first place." Remi placed her hand on Jonah's shoulder. He gave her a look that also clearly said he wasn't used to the sibling closeness. Still, he didn't pull away. "It wouldn't hurt for you to relax a little, too. Maybe spend less time worrying about those two—" she motioned to her father's room and then Josh's "—and a little more about yourself. When's the last time *you* had a fling?"

Jonah snorted. Remi was glad he hadn't taken offense to what she'd said.

"I'll have you know that I actually went out on a blind date last week, thank you very much."

Remi couldn't stop the wide grin that moved across her face.

"Oh, yeah? And how did that go?"

Jonah shrugged. It was a cocky movement.

"Must have been okay since we're supposed to meet up tomorrow."

Remi laughed and bumped her shoulder against his.

"Way to go there, Jonah boy! What's her name? Do I know her?"

He was already walking to the back door, shaking his head.

"She's new in town but, even if she wasn't, I'm not going to give you any ammo to dog me...or stalk her online."

"Oh, come on! That's not fair!" Remi followed him inside, mood lifting. It was nice to laugh with her brother. It made her forget for a moment about the insecurities swarming in her head. "How old is she? What does she do? When did she move to Overlook?"

Jonah kept shaking his head. He hurried to the stairs but paused when she threw out a last teasing insult.

"Did you know that you're a wet blanket? Has anyone ever told you that?" Remi said.

Jonah rolled his eyes.

"Her name is Lydia," he said. "And that's all you're getting."

He dashed up the stairs. Remi didn't follow. Her eyes caught on an old picture framed on the wall next to the stairs. It was of her and her father. She was sitting on a horse, her father standing next to them.

He was beaming, no doubt sure about the future.

One with his wife, his ranch, and his eldest child on a path that would certainly lead to taking over that same ranch.

But the thing about certainty was that it didn't exist.

At least, not for Remi.

She ran a hand over her stomach. Then she pulled out her cell phone.

There were no missed calls or texts.

Remi looked back at the picture for a few more moments. Then she went to bed.

Chapter Seven

Remi fell asleep next to an empty fruit-snack wrapper and woke up to Jonah looking a far cry from the humor-filled man he had been when they parted ways at the stairs the night before.

"What's wrong?" she asked, sitting bolt upright. She couldn't remember the last time Jonah had even been in her childhood room.

"You have a visitor out on the front porch," he said, his voice weirdly low. "I thought I'd give you a warning since Dad doesn't seem to much care for the Nashes and he's the one who's out there talking to him."

Remi tossed the blanket off her, threw her legs over the side of the bed and rushed to the window. Unlike her brothers' and father's rooms, hers was the only front-facing bedroom. Which meant from her window she couldn't see the covered front porch, but she *could* see the truck parked in the drive.

Declan.

It wasn't ladylike but Remi cussed under her breath. Jonah snorted and headed back for the door.

"Probably way friendlier than Dad is being to the sheriff," he said over his shoulder.

Remi didn't doubt that one bit.

She hurried to the bathroom and got presentable like it was the big triathlon she'd been practicing all year to win. Teeth brushed, face washed, mascara applied, hair detangled, and a blue flannel button-up with jeans and boots put on. She knew she could stand to be slower if she wanted. On his own Declan was already a grumpy spot for Gale Hudson. Him coming to the ranch to ask to see his daughter?

Remi bet every paycheck she'd ever made at Towne & Associates that the only way the sheriff was coming inside was if he had a warrant. And even then he might have to bust out the handcuffs to keep her father from making a scene.

December stuck to its guns on mimicking a real winter. Remi ripped her jacket off the hook by the front door and walked into the cold without properly bracing herself for it. She sucked in a breath as she tried to zip up the jacket, all while trying to gauge the situation on the porch.

Declan was standing on the bottom step, her father on the top. The latter was leaning against the railing, all casual. Declan, however, was tense. His badge had been pinned to the outside of his jacket. He greeted Remi with a smile.

It was also tense.

"Hey," Remi said, sliding into whatever conversation they'd been having. She caught Declan's gaze. "I saw your truck and thought you might be here for me?"

"And why would you think that?" her father asked so fast she got whiplash looking back at him. A heat pulsed up her neck and into her cheeks. It was born from embarrassment and quick anger.

It could have been pregnancy hormones; it could have been the fact that her father had barely said two words to her since she'd come back for the holidays.

"Because why would anyone want to visit a bunch of grumpy men holed up in one house?" she shot back, deciding it didn't matter what was fueling her sudden fire.

Her father turned, surprised but obviously ready for rebuttal. Remi was, too.

Declan went to the next step. When he spoke, his tone was so harsh that both Hudsons redirected their attention.

"I'm actually here for Jonah."

Neither Hudson said a word for a moment. Remi was too busy nursing the stab of disappointment that had pierced her. Declan hadn't called the night before and now he wasn't even there for her.

His expression softened.

"But I would like to talk to you after."

"Why do you need Jonah?" Her father had lost all illusions of being casual.

Declan's jaw was hard. He seemed to choose his words carefully.

"An incident happened yesterday involving an acquaintance of his and I'd like to ask him a few questions."

Remi shared a confused look with her father. Well,

her expression expressed *confusion*. Her father's read *defiance*.

Declan must have recognized it.

He took one more step up the stairs. When he spoke he kept her father's eye contact.

"This isn't a request, Gale."

Whether it was intentional or not, Declan shifted in his jacket, which made his sheriff's badge catch the sun's glare. It was enough to get her father moving, though he grumbled as he did so.

When Gale was back in the house, Remi descended to the step Declan was on.

"What's going on? Is Jonah in trouble? I mean he's a pain in the backside, but you know he's harmless, right?"

Declan didn't give away anything with his expression.

"He's not in trouble, but I still need to talk to him."

"You? Why not one of your detectives?" Remi lowered her voice. "Is this about the note from Well Water?"

Declan was quick to shake his head.

"It's about that call I got yesterday. I'll explain after I talk with him."

Remi's emotions fluctuated again. She couldn't help what she said next. "Will you call me like you did last night? Or should I just wait around again and hope you'll show up tomorrow instead?"

Declan's entire demeanor shifted, but she didn't have a chance to see what emotion it was shifting into.

"Remi, I——" he said but the front door opened again. Jonah came out, followed by their dad. "I want to talk to you after this," Declan finished instead. Then he met Jonah's stare with another impassive expression.

"Jonah can we talk in private for a minute?" Unlike their father, Jonah agreed without fuss. They walked out to Declan's truck and stopped by its hood.

Remi couldn't hear what they were saying as, alongside her father, she watched their body language. It changed quickly. Jonah clearly was surprised and then angry.

But not at Declan. In fact, Declan put his hand on Jonah's shoulder for a moment.

Then Jonah turned on his heel, yanked his keys from his pocket and was rushing to his car. That put Remi and her father into action. While he went to Jonah, Remi went to Declan.

"What's going on? What's wrong?"

Declan didn't seem offended or angry that Jonah was obviously leaving the conversation. He watched as Jonah quickly spoke to her dad.

"A woman was attacked in an attempted kidnapping yesterday," he explained, not mincing words. "She said she knew Jonah so I thought I'd ask him a few questions to help clarify some things for me."

Remi gasped.

"Lydia?"

"Wait. You know her?"

"I heard about her last night. Jonah went on a blind date with her. Is she okay?"

"Yeah. Shaken up and has some superficial wounds, but she's okay. Considering."

Stressed wasn't the word that described Declan in

that moment. It wasn't strong enough. The crinkles at the edge of his eyes that showed a life that had had many a laugh were woefully absent when he met her stare.

"Have you had breakfast yet? I need to eat if I have any hope of continuing to think straight."

Remi didn't have to think about it long. She hurried back to the house for her purse and phone and was sliding into the cab of his truck soon after. It wasn't until they were off Heartland that she realized they were headed toward town and not the Nash Family Ranch.

Which meant they weren't going to be alone after all.

Remi wondered if Declan had made that decision on purpose.

DOWNTOWN OVERLOOK WAS simple. A main strip with shops, eateries and slow but even foot traffic no matter the day. From the aptly named Main Street there were a few branching streets that led to a park, businesses and one that even went all the way to Second Wind, Desmond's foundation.

When Declan suggested getting something to eat, though, his mind only went to Claire's Café. It was a local favorite and run by a friend. One who, unlike most of the town, knew not to pester Declan for information when it came to a current case. Claire smiled from behind the counter after they walked in and motioned quickly to a table in the corner of the room. Partially hidden behind the pastry cabinet, it gave its patrons a slight privacy advantage while still keeping the front door in sight. Considering it was a seat-yourself establishment, that meant Claire was trying to help him out.

Which meant the town had picked up on the story of Lydia and Cooper way faster than he'd hoped.

Which *also* meant that the press conference he would be attending in two hours might not be soon enough.

"Ahh. I haven't been here in way too long," Remi said with obvious fondness. "Please tell me her home-made pecan squares are still a thing."

Declan pulled out her chair and eyed the glass cabinet near them.

"They are and it looks like she just made a new batch. You got lucky."

Remi grinned and only stood again when Claire bustled over. They hugged, said all the pleasant, polite things exchanged between old friends and then Claire dropped any guise that that was the real reason she'd come over.

"Declan, I thought you should know that all anyone was talking about this morning was Cooper and what he did to that poor woman," she said, lowering her voice so the handful of patrons already in the restaurant couldn't hear. "And, if it were me, I'd avoid talking to the new news editor of the paper. Delores doesn't say it out loud but I can tell she's having a hard time keeping Kellyn from doing the whole tabloid thing instead of using the facts."

Declan took off his hat and decided if he sighed every time he felt like it, then he might never get the chance to talk. Or breathe.

"Thanks, Claire," he said. "I'll make sure to keep a wide berth until the press conference today."

She tapped the tabletop in confirmation and went

to get them two pecan squares and two coffees. Remi changed her order to decaf before Claire could get too far away.

"I've been away a lot longer than I realized," she said. "Who are Delores and Kellyn?"

"Delores Dearborn is the editor in chief of the *Overlook Explorer* and Kellyn is the latest news editor. While we—that being me and the department—are personal fans of Delores, we're definitely on the fence about Kellyn. She likes to...*sensationalize* every story she gets her hands on. Sometimes at the expense of the facts. Delores has had her hands full keeping her on track since there aren't a lot of people at the moment who could or would want to take her place. Overlook might be a magnet for some pretty dramatic stories on occasion but it's not the most exciting place in between them."

Remi glanced at the people settled in at a few of the tables across the room.

"Like a kidnapping attempt. The same day we found a note in the wall at Well Water," she whispered.

"I'm not so sure the note even is legit anymore," he admitted. "The man who told me where the note was just so happens to be the same one who tried to take Lydia."

Remi's eyes widened in surprise.

"You think he put it there recently to—what—distract you? That seems pretty darn elaborate for something he surely could have done easier."

Declan shrugged.

"That's the only thing that makes sense right now

for me. It wasn't a secret that Dad had been working on Justin Redman's case back in the day. Picking his name to write down would definitely link back to the right time frame."

"That's all so wild." Her expression softened. "Considering I'm stressed out about this, I have to believe you're just swamped with it. How do you cope?"

Declan wanted to say he didn't. His version of coping with the stresses of the job was throwing himself deeper into that job to try to put whatever case was going on to bed. Instead, he smiled at Claire's reappearance with pecan squares and coffee. He pointed to both when she walked away.

"Sweets and coffee help."

Remi laughed. It was a light sound and it helped his mood.

It also made him feel another wave of guilt.

"Listen, Huds, I'm sorry about last night. This case just got really involved and by the time I realized what time it was I didn't want to wake you." He held up one hand in a Stop motion. "I know that's no excuse, but not calling you had nothing to do *with* you. I'm sorry."

A small smile passed over Remi's lips. It was fleeting.

"It's okay. I get it. Really, I do." She took a steady breath. Her lips, glossy and pink, parted. Declan read her body language before she spoke a word. She was about to tell him something.

Something important.

Declan didn't have a chance to find out what that something was.

Suddenly all hell broke loose outside the café. Without thought he threw himself between the rest of the café and Remi and their unborn child.

DECLAN HAD HIS gun up and out. Every patron in the room backed away from the front door. Claire, who was behind the counter with wide, searching eyes, moved behind the baked goods case. She shared a worried look with Remi.

The screeching tires and screaming had happened in an instant. Just as quickly as the appearance of Declan in front of her as a human shield. She'd barely had time to register that anything was wrong before the wall of a man was between her and the door.

Remi reached out to touch that same man, drawn to his protection like her other hand had been drawn to her stomach, linking the three of them in one fight if needed. It was a bizarre reaction Remi didn't have the time to address. When the screaming outside didn't result in an attack inside, Declan finally moved.

"Stay here," he barked over his shoulder, gun still raised.

Remi watched the door bang shut behind him but couldn't see what the commotion was through the front windows. Whatever had happened must have been just out of view.

Remi's heart hammered in her chest.

She still had her hand raised from touching Declan.

The screaming outside stopped.

But the fear rooting her feet to the ground and snaking up to her heart did not.

Chapter Eight

Declan almost mistook the bystander helping the woman as the person who had hurt her.

"Hands where I can see them," Declan ordered on reflex.

Then the details filtered in.

There were three people outside. One was an older man, gray hair haloed around a bald spot that shone in the patch of sunlight not covered by Claire's awning. He stood in the street, his full attention on the other two people outside. Which brought Declan to the younger man kneeling on the sidewalk.

He had dreads pulled back against a plaid button-up and a nice tie. They matched his pants and dress shoes. They did *not* match the blood that was on the arm of his shirt or the woman leaning against him.

Declan realized it was her scream he'd heard.

Blood, bright and angry, was smeared across her cheek. She held it with one hand and the man held her with both of his. He didn't let go as he addressed Declan.

"That man just jumped out of a car and hit her, then took off!" He motioned his head to the side.

Declan lowered his gun and followed the man's sight line, already mentally calling in backup to search the area for the man in question.

Yet, Declan couldn't believe his eyes.

A few yards away there was a man with red hair standing in the middle of the street. When he saw Declan, he smiled.

"Stop right—" Declan started to yell.

The man turned on his heel and ran like a bat out of hell.

"Call 911," he said to the man on the sidewalk.

Then he lowered his gun and dug his heels into the concrete.

Boots and dress shoes slapping the ground echoed across Main Street as the man of the hour hauled over the span of two blocks. Unlike Caleb, Declan was more muscle than speed. Unlike the man he was chasing, however, Declan was the sheriff and damned determined.

His legs burned as he pushed every muscle to eat up the distance between them. Shouts behind him filled the street as shop owners and patrons came outside to see what all the fuss was about. Declan sidestepped two bystanders with shouts to get back inside. That effort, plus yelling out for the man in question to stop, cost him a bit of endurance. But when the man hung a right around the hardware store at the intersection of Main and Juniper streets, Declan could have laughed.

Whoever the man was, he wasn't a local. Or, at least, hadn't been downtown in a while.

Tilting forward into the run, Declan curved around the corner of the building and immediately had to swerve around an orange caution cone. And then another. The intersection, sidewalk and part of the hardware store were in a construction zone thanks to a nasty spring storm that had used the trees across the street as battering rams. This week they'd started repaving the sidewalk. The road was still sectioned off.

The man didn't know that.

He cursed something awful, already halfway through a stretch of wet cement. Two cones with tape between them were knocked over. A string of workers were littered around the street and watched as Declan let out his booming voice once more.

"Sheriff's department, *stop now*!"

One man, a long-haired younger worker, sprang into action and tried to grab the culprit. Instead, he became a human shield. One that was erected so fast all Declan could do was stop and huff. The man he had been chasing grabbed the younger one and put a gun Declan hadn't yet seen against his temple, stopping them both in the wet cement.

"You stop or he dies," he panted out. He pressed the gun against the man's head again. It made him wince.

Declan didn't move his aim, but he did freeze.

"Whoa there, buddy," he tried, dropping some of the command in his voice and picking up some, as Caleb's wife said, goodwill honey. Some people responded the way Declan wanted to the commanding voice. He had a gut feeling the man with the gun across from him wasn't one of those people. "Take it easy."

He glanced between Declan and the men in neon vests along the road.

"No one do anything stupid," Declan called to them. When the man's gaze was back to him, he addressed him directly. "Drop the gun, let him go, and let's just talk. There's no need for this to go any further."

The man in question did something Declan wasn't expecting. And certainly didn't like.

He laughed.

"And what would we talk about, Sheriff?" he called. "The weather? Christmas plans? How you may be a good shot, but there's no way this would end in a good light if *you* don't put down *your* gun?"

He laughed again and then settled into a smirk.

"I'll make you a deal, though," he continued before Declan could say a word. "Throw your gun into the wet cement and I'll throw you this." He shook the young man he was holding enough to put emphasis on his control of his well-being.

A worker near Declan cussed loudly. He was older and, even with just a glance, undeniably favored the man caught between Declan and his target. It was probably his son.

Which made Declan even more uneasy at the balance of power between him and the smirking man.

"Who are you?" Declan stalled. "What do you want?"

"I'm someone who wants you to *throw your gun* into the cement."

The man didn't lose his smirk but Declan could see his patience was going as he pressed the gun harder against his hostage's head. The man winced.

Declan relented.

There were too many variables, and he didn't have the upper hand with any of them.

"Fine," he said, lowering his gun. "Just let's stay calm."

Declan's service weapon could be replaced, yet he couldn't deny he didn't like seeing it hit the light gray muck and sink in an inch or so.

He also didn't like how it felt to be that vulnerable.

There wasn't anything stopping the man from using them all as target practice.

They were at a severe disadvantage.

That is, until the younger man he held against him decided to even the playing field. He brought his elbow back so fast that Declan almost missed it.

What he didn't miss was the other man groaning out in pain as that elbow bit into his stomach. It was enough to make him lose his stance. Which also made him lose his target.

"Son of a—" The man cried out, trying to regain his composure. His captive wasn't having it. The younger man ducked and spun as much as the wet cement would allow and grabbed for the wrist of the hand holding the gun.

Declan wasn't about to wait around to see the outcome. He jumped into the cement and slogged over. He wasn't alone. Every man wearing a construction vest converged, even though the gun was still in hand.

Pride swelled in Declan's chest despite the fact that he'd much prefer there be no civilians in danger. Yet, the man who had grown up in Overlook couldn't help but be proud.

It was a feeling he carried with him as he closed the space between them with speed. Declan heard the gun hit the muck beneath them just before his shoulder connected with the attacker's chest. They sank into the cement, and Declan knew he'd won.

The man didn't fight back as Declan got to his knees and kept his hand pressed down on the man's chest.

"Don't you dare move unless I tell you," Declan ordered. The construction workers flanked him. He looked back at the discarded gun and scooped it up.

The man's head was just above the cement while his body had sunk in a bit. He smiled.

Declan didn't like when a losing man smiled.

It usually meant he didn't care enough to notice he'd lost or he hadn't actually lost at all.

A twisting thought pushed those worries aside. Declan got to his feet and the man merely pushed up on his elbows as best he could. He met Declan's gaze. In the chase and struggle, part of his shirt had drooped down around the collar.

That was when Declan saw the tattoo.

A scorpion.

The brand of the Fixers, the men and women in suits who had a reputation for being the organization other criminals called when a job was too hard to do. Or too messy to carry out.

Declan swore.

The man kept on smiling.

That twisting thought turned into a question. Declan heard the low thrum of ascending rage in his own voice as he asked it.

"Why didn't you just get back into your car after you hit that woman? Why run away if you could have driven away?"

The man was absolutely enjoying himself when he answered. It made Declan's blood run cold.

"Because, *Sheriff*, I knew the only way to get you to leave that café was if I ran."

THE WOMAN CLUTCHING at her face said her name was Rose Ledbetter. She, like Remi, the pedestrian named Sam who was holding her, and the patrons of Claire's Café, had no idea why the man had jumped out of the car to attack her and then run off. One second she had been on her way down the sidewalk and the next she'd been pistol-whipped by a stranger.

"Pistol-whipped?" Remi asked, fear flowing out of her words before her body could feel it. "He had a gun?"

Rose nodded, whimpering along with the movement. She sat at the table Remi and Declan had been sharing while the rest of the patrons crowded around. Claire was behind the counter, on the phone with the sheriff's department.

"I only saw it after he'd already hit me with it," Rose said. "I—I thought he would shoot me, but he ran instead."

"And Declan chased him."

Chased the man with the gun, she wanted to add but didn't.

Declan was the sheriff. Dealing with bad guys who had guns wasn't new to him. However, the fear uncoiling in Remi's chest was.

Declan wasn't just a boy she'd had a crush on as a girl or kissed once as a teenager. He wasn't just a man she'd shared a bed with after getting reacquainted. He also wasn't just a man who made her question if she wanted to be more than the friends they used to be.

No.

Now, and forever, he'd be the father of her kid.

No matter if they became enemies, lovers or any variation in between.

Declan Nash had cemented his place in her life the moment she'd seen the first positive pregnancy test.

And now?

Now he'd chased a man with a gun.

Normal or not, that made Remi afraid.

A feeling that must have translated into an expression she didn't have time to hide.

Sam, standing between them, looked her in the eye and was fierce with his words.

"The sheriff will be all right."

Remi gave him a small smile.

That smile died right after.

The door to the café opened with a bang. Remi already knew it wouldn't be Declan standing in the doorway, if only for the almost-violent movement, but she hoped all the same.

When she saw a man in a suit wearing a grin, a gun at his side, Remi couldn't help but suck in a breath. She wasn't alone. Everyone around her tensed.

No one spoke until the man walked farther inside. A woman in a matching pantsuit came in behind him and stopped just inside the doorway. She held her gun, aiming it at Claire.

"End the call, show me the screen, and then put it down on the counter," she ordered. Her accent was weirdly devoid of anything Remi could place. Not that it mattered. Claire was staring at a gun. She did as she was told and soon was standing with the rest of them.

The man stopped a few feet from their makeshift line next to the table. There were seven of them in total. Remi stood between Sam and Claire, Rose stayed sitting behind them.

"Don't worry, everyone," the man started. "We're not going to kill anyone as long as no one here does anything stupid."

Remi's adrenaline spiked. He didn't say anything about not *hurting* them.

"Now, let us get down to business and then we'll leave." He scanned their faces quickly, moving his head to the side to see Rose behind them. She whimpered at the eye contact.

Then he was staring at Remi.

He looked her up and down.

"Looks like you might be perfect for the job," he said conversationally.

Remi's heart was hammering in her chest.

The job? she wanted to ask. Instead, all she could do was remember to breathe as he moved directly in front of her and started to pull his gun from its holster.

"Wait a second," Sam jumped in. The man in the suit held the gun but didn't aim it. He addressed Sam but raised his voice for the crowd.

"Anyone moves and you'll make me a liar," he interrupted. "I'll end up killing you all. We good?"

Sam was tense but didn't say a word. No one did. Not even Rose's whimpers could be heard. That went double for moving.

Remi didn't want to break the only rule they'd been given, but the moment he took a step away from them and moved the gun so it was aimed at her, she had no choice.

"I'm pregnant."

The words left her mouth on a trembling plea.

Surprisingly, it seemed to have an impact. The man in the suit glanced back at his partner then to Remi.

"You're not the first person to try and lie about that."

"I have pictures on my phone," she hurried. "Of the tests. It's on the table."

There was a moment where Remi was sure trying to save herself had done the opposite. That she'd been pregnant for such a short amount of time and had already made a wrong choice as a parent. That Declan was about to suffer from another senseless act.

Yet the man sighed.

"Well, that's more trouble than it's worth," he said. He started to lower the gun. Remi felt a part of her unclench. Then the man in the suit turned to Sam. "Which I suppose means bad luck for you."

When he raised his gun and shot, Remi didn't even have time to scream.

THE SOUND OF the gunshot carried down Main Street, around the corner and right into Declan's bones. He was running before the construction workers could utter a word after him. Declan didn't care that he was leaving the man in the suit with civilians.

He had the man's gun.

What he didn't have was eyes on Remi.

Declan cursed into the wind he was creating as he ran full tilt back to the café. The gun in his hand was partially covered in cement, but he could wield it like a club if he had to. Or he'd use his bare hands.

Anything to protect the patrons he'd left behind.

Anything to protect Remi.

The ferocity of that desire should have surprised him, but he didn't have the time to dwell. Sirens started to go off in the distance, and right outside the café a car screeched to a stop. A woman ran out of the café, a man behind her.

"Stop," Declan yelled, still too far away. Pedestrians and bystanders were dotting the openings of stores and buildings along the thoroughfare, or else Declan would have tried out his new gun.

As it was, he watched as the woman ducked into the passenger side of the car and a man in a suit jumped into the back. Neither one paid attention to him; neither did the driver. Declan couldn't make out who it was as they sped off and hung a left up toward the street that ran in front of the community parking lot.

Declan looked at their license plate.

Then his focus shifted to the café.

For the first time in his career, he hesitated. With his hand on the handle of the door, he imagined the worst.

In that moment Remi was both safe and not safe. All at the same time. Just as their unborn child was unharmed and *not*. Going inside would confirm one truth. Staying outside gave him the option of keeping hope even if there was none inside.

So, for the briefest of moments, Declan hesitated.

Just as quickly he remembered that a person couldn't live in a moment. They could treasure it. They could fear it, hate it, wish to never remember it, but *staying* in a moment wasn't realistic.

It wasn't fair.

It wasn't possible.

Declan pushed open the door and saw the blood first.

Then he saw her.

Chapter Nine

The last time Remi had been in the hospital she was sixteen and, oddly enough, Declan Nash had been within
earshot. At the time he'd been with his brothers, Caleb
and Desmond, while she had been with their friend
Molly.

They'd been placed in a room outside of the ER unit
because, as Remi's father said, Declan was a wild, dangerous boy. That same wild, dangerous boy had saved
the day from the stupid yet fun game of Keep Away
with a bag of chocolate-covered peanuts during their
hike along the mountain. A hike they had gone on after
skipping school.

Remi remembered it fondly, at least the part before
they'd taken the game too seriously. Caleb had thrown
the package of candy to Molly, and Molly and Remi had
taken it too close to a sloped edge that had more tilt than
either of them realized. Remi had lost her footing first,
but Molly had let out a scream before either girl started
their slide down the leaf-covered incline.

In hindsight Remi realized that scream was probably
why Caleb had run the way he did after them, spurred

on by memories of what had happened to him, Desmond and Madi when they were younger. At the time Remi had barely hit the even ground with a groan before Caleb had lost his footing, too, and was tumbling down to meet them.

Remi remembered being terrified that she'd hurt herself enough to go to the hospital. That her father would add another notch to the post of reasons he disliked the Nash children. Yet, she'd been fine. A little bruised but no visibly broken bones or radiating pain. Though when Declan had made his way to her, he'd made her question herself. The concern in his eyes, the searching touch as his hands had seemingly been trying to find and fix whatever was hurt, and the warmth in his voice as he'd kept calm, had caused sixteen-year-old Remi to hope there was something that would keep Declan's careful attention on her.

That want had disappeared, however, when Molly and Caleb hadn't stopped their cries and grunts of pain after they were back on even ground. The walk to their vehicles had been spent trying to lay out all of their options, though they'd ultimately chosen to go with the only one that made sense.

Molly had broken her arm, Caleb had twisted his ankle, and Remi had caught lava-hot heat from her father for skipping school with her friend and a bunch of boys, Declan the Wild King among them.

Now Remi was in another room, Sam's, just off the ER in Overlook, this time older. Maybe not wiser, but with enough years between then and now to feel the full terror of a situation that could have been much worse.

When the door opened behind her, Remi didn't have time to hide the swirl of emotions starting to make her feel sick.

It was another moment of déjà vu. Declan came in, sheriff's badge on his belt and cowboy hat firmly on his head, and stopped at her side. He looked at the hospital bed and spoke to her with a lowered voice.

"I'm going to cut to the chase and tell you it's not your fault," he said. "You watching him sleep off his pain meds isn't going to do anything other than feed that guilt fire I know you've been stoking for the last two hours."

"And me pretending he didn't take a bullet that was probably meant for me isn't going to make me walk around this hospital with any pep in my step." Her words were more harsh than she'd meant them. Still, she didn't take them back.

Declan's face went a bit stony.

"All you did was tell that man you were pregnant. *He's* the one who shot Sam. Not you. I'd like to see anyone else in your shoes do anything differently." Declan motioned to Sam on the bed. He was asleep, his biceps bandaged. The damage hadn't been that bad, but Sam was a local and his friend had been the attending nurse. Remi imagined that had played into the swiftness of the pain meds he'd been given, despite his injury not being severe. It was more of a graze than anything, they'd been told. "Sam didn't blame you for what happened. No reason to blame yourself. Okay?"

Remi sighed and nodded. She followed him back out into the hallway.

Since Declan had come through the café's doors they hadn't been alone. Now, though, Remi didn't know what to say or how to act.

Seeing Declan, after he'd chased Rose's attacker, come back into the café unhurt had been a relief unlike any other. That relief seemed to be reflected in him, though Remi couldn't know how much. Chaos had erupted around them. Only now was it calming down.

Remi didn't know how to handle it so she stuck with the questions that had been piling up since the man and woman in the suits had left.

"I heard the man you chased got away?" she started in, following along with Declan as he led them down the hallway.

His body tensed. He nodded.

"After the two at the café left they hightailed it around the block and made the men holding him let go." He swore and made no looks of apology for it. "My guess was he was only meant to get me away from Claire's so the other two could go in without meeting me and my gun."

"But why? What was the point of all of that? It seems a lot of trouble to go through for not trying to steal from us or kidnap anyone."

If it was possible, Declan tensed more.

"They were making a statement."

Remi felt her eyebrow rise in question. Declan seemed to catch himself. He shook his head slightly and stopped.

"I'll tell you more later when I know more. For now I need to talk to Rose and then go back to the scene. I can get a deputy to take you home, but I thought you might like some company." He rapped his knuckles against the closed door next to them. "Since this town talks so much I figured you might want to get on top of the news." Now he looked apologetic. "And if not, I'm sorry."

Remi had a sudden fear of whoever was on the other side of the door, but it vanished as soon as it opened. Jonah gave a nod to Declan and then surprised her with a tight embrace.

"I ran into Declan in the lobby when I was at the vending machine," he said into her hair. "He told me to wait here since it was so hectic with everyone trying to get what happened straight."

Jonah pulled back and looked her up and down.

"Rusty called me and said he saw you coming out of the café with a woman who was all bloody. Are you okay?"

Remi nodded.

This was why Declan had already apologized. He must have known she wouldn't have told her family about what had happened if she could avoid it. Instead, apparently, the news was already traveling. It was best she get on top of it, starting with the closest relation to her.

She met Declan's eye. His expression was pinched. He was already getting lost in his own thoughts.

"I'll stay here, if that's okay," she said to him. Then she said to her brother, "If that's okay with you."

"I wasn't going to let you leave without telling me what's going on."

"Then this is where I'll leave you," Declan decided. He seemed to want to say more but stopped himself.

"Call me later?"

He nodded. It was a rigid movement.

Then he was gone.

Remi sighed and faced her brother. Then she realized why Jonah was there in the first place. Peeking around his shoulder she saw the covered legs of someone lying down in the bed in the center of the room.

"Is that Lydia?" she whispered.

"Yeah, she's asleep now, though. They just gave her something for the pain. She asked me not to leave her since she doesn't have anyone else in town." He smiled a little. Lydia must have left quite the impression on him.

Jonah motioned her farther inside the room and over to a couch next to the bed. Remi cringed as she saw the bandages over most of Lydia's face.

"It looks a lot worse than it is, I think," he said at her side. "But we can talk in here. I've been watching TV and it didn't bother her."

Remi settled into the seat next to him. Like being alone with Declan for the first time since everything had happened at Claire's, Remi was at a loss of what exactly to say to her brother. She loved him, she knew that, but there was more of a disconnect between them than there ever was one of understanding.

The Hudsons weren't the Nashes.

Tragedy hadn't tightly fused an already tightly fused family.

There was no triplet connection that created a unique bond between them.

There wasn't a sense of protectiveness that was forged from being in the public eye and at the center of rumors for years.

There was just a family of people who didn't understand the others' choices in life.

Which was why she became a coward when recounting what had happened at the café. Remi hesitated without an ounce of grace when she got to the reason the man in the suit had shot Sam instead of her.

She could have lied.

She could have omitted that part altogether.

She'd been caught between loving her brother and worrying at his reaction to the news that he'd be an uncle.

He wasn't an idiot. He knew something was off.

"What aren't you saying, Remi? Tell me."

She felt like sighing and then realized how much she'd been doing that lately. Acting defeated or frustrated when, given everything that had happened, she had made it out unscathed. Lucky.

Plus, she figured she'd have to tell her family at some point. Why not now?

"The reason the man in the suit shot Sam and not me was because I told him something that changed his mind." Jonah gave her a questioning look. Remi put her hand on her stomach as she finished. "I told him I was pregnant."

Jonah's eyes widened. They trailed to her stomach and then back up to her gaze.

"And was that true or were you lying?"

"It's true."

Suspicion was quick to line his expression.

"Why didn't you tell us then?"

This time Remi did sigh.

"I wanted the father to be the first to know. I told him yesterday. We were supposed to talk about it today at the café when everything happened."

Jonah had never been considered book smart—he'd rather be outside than studying—but he was well versed in common sense. Remi watched as he connected the dots from the little information he had.

When he spoke his voice rose an octave.

"Declan Nash is the father." It wasn't a question. "When you gave him a ride back to Overlook..." He shook his head. "*That's* why he came to the house personally today instead of sending his brother or a deputy. He wanted to talk to you."

Remi nodded.

"No one else knows. Well, no one else *knew*. I was going to tell you and Josh and Dad after Christmas."

"After?" A look akin to hurt passed over his face. It pushed guilt and anger to the surface for Remi.

"I figured if I told you all right before I left I wouldn't have to hear everyone complaining that long." Jonah opened his mouth to, she guessed, protest. She cut him off. "Dad hasn't liked the Nashes for a long time. He's disliked Declan, specifically, for longer. Throw in the fact that the three of you love to tell me with every other breath that I'm dishonoring my family by 'abandoning' Heartland, I thought that hiding an unexpected, out-of-matrimony pregnancy until I had an escape was a smart, sane move to make. Don't you think?"

Jonah again looked like he wanted to object but then stopped himself. He let out a long breath and nodded.

"We're not the easiest people to talk with, huh?" He gave her a small smile. Remi snorted.

"Not unless we're talking horses."

Jonah gave an identical snort. Then his expression softened.

"And how do *you* feel about being pregnant with Declan's kid?"

Remi was honest.

"Nervous, terrified and weirdly excited."

"So... I'm allowed to be excited, too, right?" he asked.

"Right."

Jonah smiled.

"You know, I've always wanted to be an uncle."

Remi couldn't deny hearing him say that was a relief. It was a feeling that relaxed the part of her that had been tense since finding out she was pregnant.

However, with one glance at Lydia, bandaged and still in the nearby bed, Remi slid fully back into her worries.

Why had the man and woman in the suits attacked Sam?

Why had the other man attacked Rose?

And when was the next attack going to happen?

THE ONLY REASON Declan went back to the hospital that night was because he knew Remi was there.

He'd spent the last several hours putting out fires their suited attackers had created. There was no keeping their brazen attacks against Rose and Sam under wraps as they'd somewhat been able to do with Cooper Mann's attack on Lydia.

And even that news hadn't been out of the spotlight for long. Declan had gone to the press conference set up for what had happened with Lydia as planned and then had to add a vague recount of that morning's chase and attacks. The news editor Claire had warned him about, Kellyn, stood on the front lines with a recorder in her hand and hungry excitement in her eyes.

For once, Declan couldn't blame her or any of the others in attendance.

If Declan hadn't been used to chaos, he would have been overwhelmed.

The note in the wall.

An attempted kidnapping.

The reappearance of a man in a suit.

Three culprits getting away.

Remi Hudson pregnant with his child.

Declan didn't count the last point as a bad one, though he couldn't deny it was heavier than the rest.

Almost as heavy as the exhaustion weighing him down as he made his way to the hospital from the department. He'd called Remi when there was nothing more he could do for the night. When she said she'd brought dinner for her brother and Lydia, Declan had changed course without a second thought.

And when she came out to the lobby to meet him, Declan did something else without a second thought.

He relaxed. If only a little.

"You okay?" he said in greeting. She didn't look tired, but she did look annoyed.

"Well, I thought I was hungry, and then I smelled the chicken I brought Jonah and it made me gag," she said in one hurried breath. "And *now* all I can think about is Pop-Tarts." Her eyes swept over him. Her pink lips turned into a line of concern. "But I shouldn't complain. How are you?"

Declan opened his mouth, fully intending to lie, and then found that the idea didn't sit well with him. Not to Remi.

So he didn't.

"I'm dog-tired." It was a simple answer and a simple truth. "I haven't gotten much sleep lately."

The corner of Remi's lips turned up into a grin. She reached her hand out, palm facing upward. Declan felt his eyebrow rise in question.

"Then you're in luck. It sounds like you need a trusted friend and confidante to take the lead for a little bit. Give me your keys and I'll drive Fiona and you back to the ranch. All the while I can regale you with some of my most harrowing accounting stories, guaranteed to help you fall into a deep, relaxing sleep." When Declan didn't immediately agree, Remi pressed on. There was an edge to her voice. "You might not be the same boy I remember on some fronts, but your stubbornness seems to be intact. Then again, so is mine. You *look* exhausted and need some sleep. I'm fine and know how to get you home. Let me."

"What about your car?" he tried.

She rolled her eyes.

"I trust it'll be just fine in the parking lot, but I'll let Jonah know so he can check on it when he leaves. Okay?"

Declan relented. He dug out his keys and dropped them onto her palm.

"Good sheriff," she said with a smile. "Now, let's go home."

She took his elbow and turned him toward the door. Through the weight of exhaustion, the best Declan could tell, Remi didn't realize what she'd said.

Her gaze remained ahead, and there was no blush in her cheeks, no hesitation in her steps.

An off-the-cuff comment that didn't mean anything past a friend taking another home.

Yet those three words had packed quite the blow.

Let's go home.

It was right then that Declan realized something.

Something big. Something life changing.

But something he wasn't going to think about just yet.

Not when the men in the suits were out there.

Chapter Ten

Declan Nash lived in a simple house furnished with simple things. Remi walked into the entry and slowly turned in a circle to take in the open floor plan. The living room was to the left, the kitchen was straight ahead, and an open archway to the right showed a small office. The door off the living room must have led to the bedroom. Declan moved to it while waving her toward the kitchen.

She'd spent most of the car ride to the Nash Family Ranch complaining about being hungry, complaining about not being able to drink more than a cup of coffee and then complaining about how cold it was getting.

Remi didn't know if it was pregnancy hormones making her grumpy or if she was looking for safe topics to talk about. Nothing that brought their future with a child into account. Nothing about the uptick in Overlook's bad-guy population. Nothing about any notes in the wall.

Just the two of them going down a dark road, her complaining about nothing in particular and him nodding along.

It was nice in a way.

Comfortable.

But now they weren't on the road.

Remi accepted his hospitality by raiding his pantry with a squeal.

"You okay?" Declan called out from the open bedroom door.

"You have Pop-Tarts," she yelled back, mouth already watering.

Declan didn't respond, and Remi settled at the small four-chair dining table set up between the kitchen and the living room couch. She was already through half of her pastry when Declan reemerged.

It was a struggle to keep her jaw from hitting the tabletop.

Remi had seen Declan naked. That was how she came to be sitting at his table, scarfing down Pop-Tarts and knowing in less than ten minutes she'd have to go pee. Again. She knew that the boy she'd grown up around had developed a firm chest and stomach and all the lines that muscles had carved in between. He even had the V that some actors and models sported in the movies and magazines. The one that led the eyes from the stomach and right down into the imagination.

She'd run her fingers along one of those very same lines, marveling that she had found herself in the situation where that touch was wanted.

After that Remi hadn't had to imagine where those lines led.

So when her lust for the sheriff went from a passive five out of ten to a red-hot, volcanic two thousand in the span of him walking through the doorway to dropping down onto the couch cushion, Remi had to double-check the scene.

Declan wasn't naked, first of all.

In fact, he'd merely swapped out his button-down and pants for a plain tee and sleep pants.

But, boy oh boy, was he wearing them.

The shirt hugged his muscled frame while the pants hung lower and a bit baggier than his jeans. It was such a casual outfit, and yet somehow sexier.

It was a glimpse into Declan behind the scenes.

A place where he could just be.

It spoke of vulnerability and it spoke right to Remi's hormones, apparently.

"I couldn't remember if I had them or not," Declan said from his spot on the couch. He leaned back, put his feet up on the coffee table and met her eyes with a smile. If she looked like an idiot, he didn't say it. Even when she scrambled to look normal while finishing her bite of Pop-Tart. "I babysat Riley's nephew the other week and that boy was all about some frosted strawberry. I didn't really think about it until we were in the car."

Remi held up the uneaten portion in a salute.

"Well, I thank you for it."

Declan seemed satisfied that she was satisfied and leaned his head back, put his arms over his chest and closed his eyes.

"I'm sorry I'm so tired," he said after a yawn. "Sometimes I forget that I need to recharge, even though I tell Caleb and my deputies to do it all the time." His eyes opened again, but there was a lag to the movement. He didn't move his head as two grass-green eyes found hers.

Remi put her food down. She felt a tug at her heart-strings. Declan Nash might not be a great talker, but when he did speak he managed to put a whole lot into what he said. Simple statements, yet with so much depth they were nearly overwhelming for Remi to hear, especially when she thought of the always-smiling and mischievous boy she'd once kissed on a dare beneath the moon and stars when she was nothing more than a quiet girl.

The time after they'd parted ways had been kind to him in some respects, but Remi believed it had also run him down in others.

And then he said as much to her utter surprise.

"My dad always used to say that even though there's never enough time to do everything you want to do, there's always time to do at least one thing. Just make that one thing count." He let out a small breath and domed his fingers over his lap. Remi realized she was hanging on his every word. "I didn't think I had a *one thing* for years until I met Bobby Teague."

The name rang a bell.

"The mayor when we were teens?"

Declan shook his head.

"His son," he replied. "Not the nicest man, not the most patient, either. I didn't like him, just like his dad hadn't liked mine back in the day. They were men who wanted attention and became annoyed when they actually got it. A son who became an even grumpier version of his father. And then a pain in my backside. Then one day Bobby Teague came into the department with nothing but fear in him. His sister had gone on a date and hadn't returned to her house." Declan sat up a little. The frown of remembering settled into his lips as he took a moment. "It hadn't been twenty-four hours yet so we couldn't count it as a missing person but, well, after what happened to the triplets, the rules for missing persons in Wildman County are a bit different. I wasn't waiting around hoping that his sister was fine and was just lost in a new love bubble. And Bobby refused to be sidelined. So, he rode with me as we went all over town looking for her."

Remi saw the subtle shift in the man, though she couldn't place the emotion behind it.

"It took us a bit to track down where her date lived, but when we did everything changed between me and Bobby. His digs at me and my family, his sarcasm and ego getting into every word he said, it just all went away the moment we got to the end of that driveway. One second we were two people who didn't much like each other. Nothing in common. No love lost at all between us. And in the next, we were two people who wanted nothing more than for Lori Teague to be okay and would do anything to see that happen."

His words were tired and the rest of what he wanted to say seemed to stall out. Remi hated to prod the man, but she wanted to know what had happened.

"Was she there? At the date's house?"

"She was and she was fine, too," he said with a small smile. "Her phone had died so she hadn't gotten any of the calls and then she lost track of time…doing what happens with some dates, if you catch my drift."

"I do."

"It was a good call. One that could have turned out much worse. Weirdly enough, *that* was when I realized what it was that I wanted to be my *one* thing." Remi leaned in as Declan's expression hardened, resolute. "Making sure people like Bobby Teague didn't have to spend their lives worrying. Instead, they could sigh in relief or, ideally, never have the need." Declan shrugged. "So I threw everything I had into my career, to Overlook, to the county. I woke up worrying about everyone and went to bed wondering how I could make their lives better."

A vulnerability that Remi hadn't been prepared for took over the sheriff. Not only did it pull at her heartstrings, it made something else within her stir.

"When you told me you were pregnant, I didn't act the way I should have. Running off to work, losing track of time and not calling, and then pulling you back into trouble… I should have said, and done, more. It's just… Well, I think I've been so focused on what everyone else wants and needs for so long that, along the way, I forgot to wonder what it is I want."

Every part of Remi went on alert. She could have sworn if a pin had dropped in between his earlier words, she could have heard it as easily as if a bowling ball had been dropped onto the hardwood.

"And what do you want?" she chanced.

The father of her unborn child smiled.

"I know I want to be a part of my kid's life, from now

until I'm old, gray, and then in the grave. Everything else? Well, I'm just too tired to think about any of that right now." His mood darkened. He didn't need to say it but Remi knew his thoughts had found their way back to Cooper Mann and then the attack and chase at Claire's.

It was the only reason she didn't push him for more.

And the only reason she didn't give any of what she wanted to say back.

Instead, Remi tried to be reassuring.

"No one has their entire life planned out. You'll have plenty of time to figure out what's next for you. Until then, why don't you go get some sleep."

Declan snorted. He kicked his feet up and swung his legs over onto the couch. Then he slid down against the cushions with a sigh. It reminded Remi of when she slid into a much-needed warm bubble bath.

"I'm good right here," he said, his eyes closing. "Feel free to eat whatever else you want. There's a spare toothbrush in the cabinet over the sink and some more pj's in the dresser."

That surprised Remi.

"You want me to stay?"

He nodded, eyes still closed. Then he yawned.

"I can't make you but I'd feel better if you were close. Last time I—" He yawned again. This one was deeper, longer, too. The man was dancing near the edge of sleep, there was no denying it. "Last time I left you all hell broke loose. Not gonna happen again. Bed's yours."

Remi smiled into her Pop-Tart. Then she remembered something she needed to tell the man before sleep claimed him.

"Hey, Declan. I told Jonah about the baby in the hospital today."

Declan opened his eyes.

"Did you tell him I'm the father?"

"I did."

Declan surprised her with a nod and a simple response.

"Good."

Remi smiled. Declan returned it. Then his eyes closed and, just like that, Declan quieted. By the time Remi had finished her Pop-Tarts the man was sound asleep.

THE HOUSE WAS different in winter.

The heater made it smell like something was burning sometimes. Not like an all-out fire or anything but more of a lingering firepit smell that always reminded Declan of the day after a bonfire had burned out. That smell, rare since Declan hardly ever turned the heater on in the house, combined with the lack of noise he was used to surrounding the ranch, sometimes disoriented him when he first woke up. It didn't matter that he'd had just as many years knowing winter in Overlook as he'd known summer. There was just something about the cold outside that threw off his internal navigation and understandings.

Like when he opened his eyes to the darkness, smelled something burning and heard something he wasn't used to hearing.

Declan sat up so quickly he nearly pulled a muscle.

It was dark in his immediate area, but on the other side of the room there was a soft glow. That light was enough to show him a space he knew. It clicked in place with the smell of the heater and the feel of the couch beneath him.

And the old wool blanket he was particularly fond of that he'd thrown to the ground in half-asleep earnestness.

He rubbed at his eyes and then worked at blinking away the haze of sleep. Wondering what had wakened him, he turned toward a window. Through the open slats of the blinds he could just make out another glow, though this one wasn't as focused.

It was dawn, and Declan bet that routine had been the thing that had wakened him. He'd never quite shaken waking up early on the ranch as a kid, especially when school was out. As the oldest child he'd had the most to do. Now he normally used the time to go on a run or drink coffee and worry.

He snorted in the dark.

I sure am exciting, he thought ruefully.

His gaze returned to the soft glow nearest him. The one that he knew came from his bedside lamp in the bedroom. Moving slowly, careful to be quiet, Declan got up, went to the open doorway and looked inside.

Dark blond hair was splayed across a navy pillowcase while the covers he hadn't gotten beneath in days housed a woman wearing his clothes.

Remi.

She'd stayed.

Her face, slack with sleep, was turned toward Declan, as beautiful as when she was awake.

And what do you want?

Declan hadn't meant to come clean with what he was feeling the night before. He hadn't meant to admit he'd had tunnel vision with his job the last several years. Just as he hadn't meant to say that her news had finally made him confront the fact that he'd forgotten about himself in the grand scheme of things.

He'd honestly just been tired as hell and ready to fall asleep so he could start fresh in the morning. Yet, when he'd seen Remi sitting at the dining table eating a pack of Pop-Tarts of all things, Declan hadn't been able to stop himself. He'd seen the woman just as he'd seen the girl who had once been his friend.

He'd felt comfortable. So, he'd opened up.

What he *had* meant to say was his realization that, no matter what his future held, he knew without a doubt he wanted it to include their child. It was just a declaration he'd hoped to make in better circumstances, not in his sleep pants after a majorly crappy day.

Also, not immediately before he'd fallen asleep.

But there she'd been and there he'd told her.

And now there she was, asleep in his bed.

It wasn't a new sight for Declan to see her asleep. One time he'd seen her drift off at a school assembly, bored out of her mind. Lon McKinnley had tried to pull her hair to wake her then, so Declan had thumped the boy on the head and dared him in silence to do it again.

What *was* new was how it felt to watch her do so.

The urge to join her was almost as strong as the urge

to run a hand across her cheek and tuck behind her ear the strands of hair that had escaped. To feel the warmth of her skin. To feel the smoothness. To—

Adrenaline shot through Declan's bloodstream. It zipped his spine straight and had him retreating into the living room to look for his phone.

Shame, deep and biting, mingled with the new sense of urgency.

How had he not put together the pieces before?

How had he been so blind to not understand what was going on?

Declan cussed, low and with vehemence.

How had he not seen the pattern until now?

Rose hadn't been targeted, per se, but her face had.

Sam wasn't the plan, getting shot in the arm was.

Just like Madi and Caleb.

The day they had been abducted.

Chapter Eleven

"He's not going to figure it out," the woman whined. Her name was Candy and, unlike it, she was not at all sweet. She'd spent the entire car ride back complaining that she hadn't been the one to shoot the man or hit the woman or even put a gun to the other man's head.

Candy was what some professionals might call a sociopath. For him, he thought of her as nothing more than a nuisance.

"He'll put it together," he assured her. "He's smart."

She snorted.

"He sure didn't seem like a man who had put it together at the hospital. He just stood there and made puppy dog eyes at the pregnant chick from the café."

"Remi Hudson," he interjected.

Candy cocked her head to the side at that.

"Hudson? As in—"

He nodded, not needing her to finish the thought.

"The very same."

Candy, for once, looked slightly satiated. It never lasted. Her need to always be doing *something* was a big part of why she'd been chosen to join him.

She rarely shied away from what they needed to do.

"Well, while this has some potential to finally be interesting, it won't matter at all if our dear sheriff doesn't put any of the pieces together. Why leave bread crumbs if the idiot won't ever follow them?"

He sighed.

"He's dealing with a lot. Give the man a few beats. He'll get to where we need him."

Candy's eyebrow rose in thinly disguised disgust.

"You sound like you're fond of the eldest Nash. Then again, I've heard you have a soft spot for all of the Nash kids. Had several chances to take them out over the last few years and now look where we are. Here, waiting for a man to find breadcrumbs."

Unlike some of the men and women he surrounded himself with, *he* kept his cool, even if he would have liked nothing more than to tell the woman off. Point out her brazen attitude would only ever get her, and maybe him, killed. That she might have joined them two years ago, but she was nowhere near his level.

"It wasn't my job to kill them, just like it's not my job to kill Declan now," he said, keeping his voice as crisp as the chill outside of the building above them. "I come up with plans and I follow plans. *That's* how I serve this organization and *that's* how I stay off the radar and alive."

"Whisperer."

He snorted at the moniker he'd been given by the men and women within their group. One that hadn't yet made it to any law enforcement ears.

"There's something to be said about the power of

suggestion." He lost all humor. "Just like there's something to be said about the Nash family." He leaned across the table enough to focus her attention. Candy lost her humor, too. She might have been insolent nine times out of ten, but for that one time she knew when to bite her tongue and listen. "In the last few years people, for whatever reasons, have taken their cracks at them. Threatened them, attacked them, tried to hurt them and the people they loved. Now, answer me this…" He ran a thumb across the raised skin on his hand, a scar he'd had for years. "Who's still standing? The people who went after the Nashes or the Nashes themselves?"

Candy didn't answer.

She didn't have to because they knew exactly who had come out on top in those encounters.

"Respecting the enemy means you don't underestimate them," he added. "A lesson you might want to learn."

Candy opened her mouth, but approaching footsteps kept the words back. The man who filled the doorway next demanded quick respect with his silence.

Even more with the pointed stare. He addressed Candy, who tried her best to look as if she wasn't afraid of him.

"Go tell Hawthorne to shut up about today. You two keep bragging like you've done something a child couldn't easily do. Go."

Candy didn't sneer or back talk him or try to be clever. She fled the room like her life depended on it.

And maybe it did.

Depending on his mood, their boss could be a very *difficult* person to be around.

Still, when it came to the boss he wasn't like Candy. His fear of the boss was surrounded by a thin protective layer that had been built over time.

They had something in common.

Something none of the others had.

That didn't stop him from being worried that the boss was standing in front of him.

"I heard about yesterday. You did a good job." He came closer but didn't sit down. "I also heard that you didn't use Miss Hudson because she said she was pregnant."

"It was a complication I wanted to avoid. Once she said it out loud, it didn't matter if she was pregnant or not, that kind of news might have inspired someone else in the café to be a hero. I didn't have the time for it."

The boss nodded.

"I would have made the same call. No sense in muddling the message with unnecessary drama. But, as it turns out, she *is* pregnant." His expression transformed into something he hadn't seen in a long, long time. Glee. "With Declan Nash's child."

"You've got to be kidding me."

He shook his head with a little laugh.

"She told her brother in the hospital after yesterday's events."

For a moment the two marveled at the news. Then the boss slowly hardened back into the determination that had been driving him for over two decades.

"Using Declan was always a risk. Miss Hudson has

taken that risk out entirely. We get her, we get him. The other Nashes will follow, trying to save the day." He moved back to the doorway, his mind no doubt already spinning a revision to his plan. Even though they'd gone over every variation there had been to it, every possible outcome, every contingency they could think of, the hair on the back of his neck stood on end when the boss got to the bottom line. The endgame. The only reason they were all there.

"Then we'll kill them all."

Chapter Twelve

Madi Nash had a thin scar across her cheekbone.

Caleb Nash had a scar across his upper arm from a bullet graze.

Desmond had a limp that would never fully heal.

Cooper Mann had none of the above. The only affliction he seemed to have was that he tended to be more nerves than anything else. Like right now, through the bars of a Wildman County cell. His eyes were wide and tired. He'd seen better days and it showed.

Instead of pleading his case, repeating over and over that he hadn't tried to take Lydia Cartwright, he simply watched Declan stop just outside of the bars. Even as Declan studied him, the young man remained quiet.

"Cooper, do you know what I did this morning before I got here?" Declan started. He didn't wait for Cooper to try to guess. "I went out to the impound lot and took a look at your car because something just isn't sitting right with me. You know what I found? An oddly clean car, leather seats that were well taken care of, and a CD player. I can appreciate you having one because I know that isn't the standard with newer cars, but I just

have to question the CD that I found *in* it." Declan recalled the name from memory with a slight head tilt in
question. "*How to Learn Spanish in Three Easy Steps.*
It was on the third track of five and in the middle of a
lesson. Were you listening to it before you got out of
the car and saw Lydia?"

Cooper's eyes flitted from one side of the room to
the other. He didn't move off the cot he'd been sitting
on as he answered.

"Yeah, I was."

"Can I ask why?"

"Because I'm trying to learn Spanish," Cooper dead-
panned. Declan almost laughed. He'd sure walked into
that one.

"No. I mean, *why* are you trying to learn Spanish? Is
it something you've been wanting to do for a while now
or something you tried on a whim?" Cooper straightened. He crossed his arms over his chest, defensive.
Declan sighed. "Cooper, I left a beautiful woman at
my house and in my bed to go to the lot before hours
to check your car and now I'm here. The case against
you is already as damning as damning can be. Lydia
Cartwright swears up and down that you are the man
who attacked her. Answering me now, about a CD in
your car, isn't going to do any more harm. Not answering will only make me grouchier than I already am."

Cooper seemed to weigh his options.

"A beautiful woman," he said. Declan thought he
was repeating him and then realized it was an answer.

"A beautiful woman is why you're trying to learn
Spanish?"

Cooper nodded.

"Her name is Inez. She works at Waypoint as one of the bartenders." He sighed deeply. It deflated him. "It was love at first sight for me. Dark hair, dark eyes, and this laugh thing she does when she's brushing drunk guys off. Most beautiful woman I ever saw."

"Have you asked her out?" Declan prodded when the man trailed off.

"Yeah," Cooper exclaimed with sudden vigor. "I sure did! And do you know what she said? 'Ask me in Spanish and then we'll talk.' Can you believe that?" Even though his voice was raised in frustration, it was clear he wasn't angry at the bartender. In fact, when he spoke again it was akin to being impressed. "Nothing worth having is ever easy, though, is it? I ordered the CD since I like driving around a lot. Was hoping to go back this coming weekend and show off but…" Cooper's face fell. Any and all feeling he'd had went with it. He didn't bother finishing his thought.

Sympathy started to sprout in Declan's chest. A seed that had always been there, watered by Cooper's story.

One that was growing now.

"Cooper Mann, come over here and look me in the eye," he barked, a little more forcefully than he meant.

But it did the trick.

Cooper hopped up and came to the bars. Through them he met Declan's stare.

"Why would you try to kidnap Lydia Cartwright if you were so worried about learning Spanish to ask out the most beautiful woman in the world this weekend?"

Cooper might have been nervous and he might have been scared, but he answered with a steady voice.

"I wouldn't."

And, by God, if Declan didn't believe him.

THERE WAS A package of Pop-Tarts on the kitchen counter with a sticky note stuck to it. Declan said he was sorry for leaving, but he'd gotten her car to his house and he'd call her later.

Remi was both let down and touched.

She changed back into her clothes, pocketed the pastries and decided it was time to go to Heartland.

While Jonah had promised to keep the pregnancy under wraps until she told Josh and their father, she remembered how bad Jonah had been at keeping secrets when they were younger. He had too much honor when it came to their father. He snitched quicker than Josh could gallop between the stables and Heartland's outer fence.

Which was pretty damn quick.

Remi still hadn't completely forgiven him for blabbing about the belly button piercing she'd gotten with her friend Molly in high school.

That fallout had lasted a good while.

At least now she couldn't be grounded.

There were clouds in the sky and the air was cold. Remi pulled up beside Josh's truck and could see her father's and Jonah's off to the side of the house. She decided dawdling wasn't going to make anything easier.

She took a deep breath, pushed out into the cold, and

didn't make it two steps into the house before Jonah appeared.

"I told him you stayed at Molly's," he hurried in greeting. "I didn't know how you wanted to handle everything with the, you know, so I kind of panicked."

Despite her earlier annoyance, Remi laughed.

"Afraid he'll find out I was bunking with Declan?" she asked, lowering her voice. "Do you think he'd be worried I'd, I don't know, gotten pregnant?"

She gave him a look that showed she was teasing.

Jonah rolled his eyes but smiled.

"Listen, I'm just trying to keep the peace before you break it. Can't blame a guy for trying."

Remi started up the stairs.

"I blame whoever I want for whatever I want," she said, grinning. "Don't you forget that, Jonah Bruce."

Remi bounded up the stairs to the sound of Jonah being annoyed and locked herself in her room. One thing that had been a surprise for her about pregnancy so far was how energetic she was during some parts of the day. Like now she felt as if she'd already had an entire cup of coffee on top of eight hours of sound sleep. She knew these moments didn't always stick. Exhaustion and fatigue were always waiting around the corner, ready to strike. That had been her mother's only major symptom when she'd been pregnant. Remi hoped it would be the same for her going forward.

Then again, she wasn't holding her breath for that.

Remi took her prenatal vitamins, ate the Pop-Tarts on her bed and then went to take a nice, long shower. Her mind wandered to days when she was younger and her biggest concern was trying to keep her grades up and then right over to seeing the man in the suit shoot Sam.

She left the shower in a less good mood than when she'd gotten in.

Jonah and Josh were in the living room. One was reading, the other on his laptop.

"It's a rare sight to see you two inside," she noted. Jonah snorted. Josh was more direct. He always was, despite being the youngest. He had more of their mother in him than the rest of them.

"Until we get the ranch back to how it was, there will be a lot more downtime than what you remembered from when you last called this place home," he said, close to sneering. It made Remi's adrenaline spike in a flash of anger.

"This is my home as much as it is yours. Just because I left doesn't mean I didn't grow up here, same as you."

Josh pushed his laptop onto the couch cushion next to him.

"And just because you're visiting for the holidays doesn't mean we've forgotten how happy you were to leave in the first place. And how often you *don't* visit when it's not the holidays."

Guilt stabbed Remi quickly in the chest. Her anger overcompensated. She dropped her voice low, seething.

"And how often will you visit after you've skipped town with your one true love?"

Josh looked like a deer in the headlights. When he recovered, his expression matched her mood. He turned it on Jonah.

"You told *her*?"

Jonah abandoned his book.

"That *her* is our sister," Jonah defended. "Wouldn't you rather me tell *her* than Dad?"

Josh didn't have to chew on that question long. But that didn't mean he was ready to roll over. He whipped his head around to her so fast Remi was surprised it didn't pop right off.

"If you tell Dad so help me—"

"So help you what?" Remi interrupted. "Are you threatening me, baby brother? What you and the other two Hudson men keep seeming to forget is that before *'my betrayal of house and home'* I got to see you grow up, too." She laughed. It was unkind. "I saw you try to fight Marlin Crosby. Operative word, *try*."

Josh's face changed to the color of her cherry bomb lipstick.

"Marlin Crosby cheated," he said, frustration at the humiliating fight ringing clear through every word. "He rushed me when I was talking to *you two*!"

Remi took several steps forward, putting her into the same orbit as her brothers. Men might have been sitting a few feet from her, but all she saw were the little boys who used to annoy her to no end. Little boys playing at being adults while she had already graduated.

"He hit you from behind because you were too busy telling us, and everyone else watching, how you were going to beat him up. He didn't win because he cheated. He won because your mouth is bigger than your brain!"

That did it. That activated her younger brother like flipping a switch. He jumped up, face as red as ever, and she reacted by squaring her shoulders, ready to wrestle like they had done when they were kids.

"Whoa there!" Jonah was faster than either one of them. He put his body between them and hands out on Josh's chest.

Remi was ready to knock both of them silly, absolutely done with their talk of her abandoning her family because she had had the *audacity* to live her own life, but the sound of boots against hardwood silenced them all.

Gale Hudson filled the doorway between the living room and the kitchen. He must have come in through the back door and they hadn't heard him because, in hindsight, Remi realized they'd been yelling awfully loud.

"I can't ground you like I used to," their father started, voice always booming. "But I can sure enough make life harder for the lot of you if you don't stop your bellyaching. You hear me?"

All three Hudson children took a breath and relaxed their tensed muscles.

"Yes sir," they sang in a chorus.

Their father nodded, satisfied.

"Good. No one should be fighting this close to Christmas, if nothing else. What is it that your mom used to say about it?"

"Fighting on Christmas will only get you the present of shame," Jonah recalled. However, there was still some kick in Josh.

"She meant that about Christmas Day, not the rest of them."

"Well, then, I'm making an amendment," their father said. "No fighting during December."

This time it was Remi who decided to try her luck.

"Can I add 'no guilting your children for their life choices' to the list?"

"Remi," Jonah whispered in warning.

Their father, however, surprised them. He chuckled.

"Your mom used to say you reminded her of herself, but there's a lot of times I hear my stubbornness come out of your mouth." His expression softened. "Instead of you all yelling, why don't we make an early lunch and eat together? It's been a while."

And just like that all the tension left the room.

"Brunch," Remi said, following him into the kitchen.

"What?"

"It's called brunch. A meal between breakfast and lunch."

"Sounds like nonsense to me."

Remi laughed and soon the four of them were moving around the kitchen, preparing whatever food was in the fridge. It was nice. Their father started to complain about a horse they were boarding whose owner wouldn't stop calling him, while Josh pointed out that that was probably because she had a crush on him. Remi and Jonah were paired up to the side of the refrigerator and cringed at the news that someone had a crush on *their* dad when Josh slid a plated sandwich to her. It was and had been her favorite since she was a kid. A peace offering in the form of turkey, jalapeños, cheese and wheat bread.

Remi hesitated. Not because of the surprising offer

but because she couldn't accept it. She didn't know a lot about pregnancy yet, but she did know she couldn't eat sandwich meat.

Jonah bumped her shoulder, a questioning look on his face.

She pointed to her stomach and shook her head.

He pointed to his plate. Leftover chicken potpie. *His* favorite.

Remi nodded.

If Jonah had accepted her pregnancy this fast, what was stopping her from giving the other two Hudson men the same chance to do the same?

Because old wounds don't heal just like that.

Remi might have gotten lucky with Jonah but that didn't guarantee it would be as easy with the others. So, she decided to keep stalling a little while longer. At least she could wait until she had a full stomach.

Her and Johan were in the middle of switching meals when an odd sound filled the house.

The doorbell.

For a moment they all looked at one another as if to say, *We're all here so who is using the bell?* Everyone who frequented the ranch knew to knock because their dad hated the bell.

Except for Declan. He had no idea.

"I'll get it," Remi said, hurrying past the boys before they could answer it. Remi's phone was in her back pocket. She brought it out to check to see if she had a missed call or text from the man.

She hadn't.

And it wasn't him at the door, either.

Remi opened the door wide as soon as she saw the angry tears and stitches across the woman's face.

"Lydia?"

The last time Remi had seen the woman was right before she and Declan had left the hospital. The doctors had said she was being discharged but probably not until that afternoon. Jonah had told her he'd pick her up from the hospital himself when that happened.

Now there she was on their doorstep, wearing a blouse with blood on it and jeans that had a tear. It must have been the same outfit she'd been wearing when she was attacked by Cooper Mann.

It was a jarring sight. Made even more so by the fact that the woman didn't seem bothered by any of it.

"Hi there, Remi," she greeted in return. "Do you think I could come inside?"

"Oh, yeah, of course." Remi might have been thrown off her game, but she hadn't lost her manners. She stepped aside, waving Lydia into their home.

"Jonah is in the kitchen," she said, already moving that way. Lydia shook her head.

"I'm not here for Jonah," she said.

"Oh?"

Lydia smiled.

It should have been a red flag.

It should have been a lot of things.

What it wasn't was enough to make Remi use the phone in her hand to call for help.

Instead she listened, intently, for the reason.

"I'm here for you."

Chapter Thirteen

Lydia struck out before Remi could move a muscle.

The hit landed against her chest, just below the collarbone. It hurt. Remi staggered backward from the force and surprise. She didn't have a chance to catch herself. Her backside hit the hardwood just as her periphery was filled with the bulk of her father and Jonah.

They hadn't seen the hit.

Remi heard her father say her name just as Jonah called out to Lydia. Neither had a chance to finish their thoughts or get answers in return.

Lydia pulled out a gun and aimed it at the men.

Remi reacted on reflex.

From her angle on the floor she couldn't do much, but she was close enough to do something. She brought her fist up and paid the woman in kind for the hit she'd been given. But Remi could only get as high as her stomach from where she was on the ground.

It did the job well enough.

A gunshot exploded inside the house, pushing pain through Remi's ears at the sound just as fear rang through her heart, but Lydia gasped for different reasons.

She hadn't counted on the hit to the stomach, just as Remi hadn't counted on the hit to the chest.

Lydia stumbled but didn't fall. She kept the gun but lost her aim.

Remi took advantage of the distraction. She pushed up off the ground and right into the woman. Lydia completely lost her footing this time. Like a rag doll, the woman fell back and out onto the front porch.

Then Remi did the only thing her adrenaline and slightly good sense would let her do.

She slammed the door shut and threw the dead bolt.

The sound of Lydia cursing became the soundtrack behind the next important, life-altering thing in Remi's world. She turned, heart in her throat, and hoped to every god there ever was that none of her family had been shot.

Her father was rushing over to her. Josh and Jonah watched wide-eyed from the doorway.

No one was bleeding, no one was on the ground.

It was a relief that didn't last long.

"Get away from there," her father grunted out, grabbing her wrist. Another explosion went off as Lydia shot through the door. It barely missed them as her father slung Remi around and pushed her to the stairs. Remi didn't hesitate in running up them, out of line of the door.

"Stay low, boys," he yelled over his shoulder.

Remi hit the landing as another gunshot went off. It was followed by two more. She spun on her heel, but her father pushed her farther onto the second floor.

"There's a gun in my room," he said. Remi would

have marveled at how calm he was being if not for the directive he gave her as he pulled her along with him to the bedroom at the end of the hall. "Call for help, Remi. Do it now."

Remi went for her phone only to have her stomach drop. Just as she had done with her phone after being hit by Lydia.

"I—I don't have it." She heard it then. In her voice. A waver of terror, strengthened by adrenaline and confusion.

They ran into the master bedroom and made a U-turn to the closet.

"That's okay." He was using his soothing voice. The one she'd once heard when she'd accidentally cut her hand with a knife and needed stitches. He'd brought her nerves down simply by the cadence of his voice.

Whether or not he agreed with her leaving town, there was a comfort in knowing that, with just the sound of his voice, her father could make her feel better.

"What about the landline?" she asked, hopeful. It didn't last long.

"I took the cordless to the kitchen yesterday. Haven't put it back."

Remi doubled back to the bedroom door as her father opened his safe in the closet. He'd always been diligent about keeping all weapons locked up, even when his children had grown, but what he had in there Remi had no idea.

She watched the hallway and the top of the stairs with a twist in her gut. Her brothers hadn't attempted to go for the second floor. She hoped they had fled through the back door as soon as the shots kept coming and that one of them had called for help.

"The front door open yet?" her father asked, rushing back to her side.

They both paused.

The house around them was eerily silent.

Remi opened her mouth, ready to call for her brothers, but her father grabbed her wrist.

"Shh, keep quiet," he whispered. "We don't know if she's alone or not, and we don't want to let her know exactly where we are."

He had shut the bedroom door and locked it when two things happened at once.

First, she heard glass shatter downstairs. The living room windows maybe.

Then she felt a peculiar wetness against her arm.

"I need you to listen to me," her father said, but Remi stopped him when she realized what that wetness was.

"You're bleeding."

The last few shots hadn't missed them.

At least, not her father.

"I'm okay," he tried, pulling her again. The wetness grew against her arm. He stopped when they were in the en suite, and turned to shut and lock the door.

Remi turned her attention to his bullet wound.

"Dad."

There was no denying he'd been hit. His button-up was turning dark at the side of his stomach. He was trying—and failing—to keep his left forearm pressed against it.

"I'm okay," he repeated.

Remi was devastated to hear the waver in his voice this time.

Instead of fear, she heard pain.

He swung around and showed her something else she hadn't had the mind to notice yet. It was a revolver. He held it out to her. Remi took it with a sob stuck in her throat.

"Do you remember how to use that? No safety and no cocking it between shots. Just shoot. Understood?"

"I don't want to use it. I want *you* to use it."

He shook his head and moved to the window.

"If there's more than one of them and they come up here, I want you to use the lattice next to Josh's room to get down to the ground. Then, only if it's clear, make it to the stable. That's where you're all supposed to go if bad stuff happens in the house. Josh and Jonah will be there."

Remi watched, her heart nearly crushed with helplessness as the strongest man she knew fell against the wall and slid to the floor.

"Dad." It was all Remi could do not to yell. She knelt down in front of him, the hand not holding the revolver, trying helplessly to grab onto a part of him as if her touch alone could help heal him.

It did no such thing.

Dark eyes searched her face. His expression softened, but his words were stern. Harsh.

"That was a good move you made with that woman downstairs, but bullets count for more than courage. You can take on one person—don't try to take more if there are more. Promise me, Remi. You run if there's more than one person out there and use that thing to protect your brothers. Don't be afraid to shoot."

Then he gave her that look.

That look of unconditional love. The same one her mother gave them. The same one her grandmother had given her mother before she'd passed away.

The love of a parent for a child.

The same love Remi already felt for hers.

She nodded.

And then, in the simplest of terms, she told her father the news she should have already told him.

"I'm pregnant."

Gale Hudson took all of two seconds to respond.

"Shoot to kill, baby girl."

Remi wanted to say more, to *do* more, but an awful sound cut off any conversation.

Wood splintered. A thud sounded.

Then a man spoke. Followed by another.

"We know you're in there," he yelled.

It wasn't her brothers.

Which meant Lydia wasn't alone.

Which meant Remi was supposed to abandon her father.

The doorknob shook.

Her father touched her stomach. Blood transferred to her shirt, but he got his point across with it.

He was trying to protect her.

And it was her turn to do the same for her child.

Remi looked at her father one last time and then slid the window up. She was up and out of it within a breath. Her shoes hit the roof that hung over the wraparound porch. The backyard was, at a glance, empty. No one shot at her. No one yelled.

She ran.

Josh's room was at the corner of the house. Attached to the overhang outside of his window was a thick lattice their mother had built herself. She'd wanted it for decoration. Her children had used it to sneak out of the house.

Now her daughter was using it to escape.

Why was Lydia there for her?

Who were the men?

Were there more?

Remi didn't have any answers. She knew only that she didn't want to find them by letting Lydia get ahold of her or her brothers. Sibling protectiveness combined with maternal protectiveness drove Remi's hands and feet as she got to the edge of the roof outside of Josh's room and onto the top of the lattice.

She slipped twice as she tried to find footholds not completely covered in vines, then dropped the last two feet to the ground. Pain radiated up her shins but she didn't stop.

Hudson Heartland had several stables. Some were at the front of the acreage, others were tucked toward the back. The stable they had been taught to go to if there was ever a fire, break-in or other disaster in the main house was a faded red barn a hundred yards or so from the back porch. It had housed Heartland's personal horses and had never been used by clients.

It also had a landline.

Remi ran full tilt toward it, knowing if anyone was

on the roof or in the bathroom looking out, they'd see her. If anyone came after them they could just keep running until they made it to the woods.

The Hudson children knew the ranch.

She doubted Lydia and whoever was with her could claim the same.

At least, that was her hope as she struggled to breathe while running away from the house.

From her father.

Remi ignored the ache in her heart.

She had to protect her brothers.

She had to protect her baby.

"LYDIA CARTWRIGHT DIDN'T exist until five years ago."

Declan should have felt something at hearing the words out loud, but a part of him was going on autopilot. A routine created out of necessity for being sheriff. A detached acceptance of what he was learning. A bridge between throwing his hands in the air with anger and confusion and complete silence. An in-between where he could stay for a while until he figured out how he needed to, as sheriff, react to whatever news he received.

Caleb ran a hand through his dark hair and then hung his hand on the detective's badge on a chain around his neck. Jazz was sitting in the chair he was hovering over while both looked at the computer screen.

"Why do you say that?"

Caleb touched the computer screen, but Declan couldn't see what they were looking at.

"First of all, that's when all of her social media accounts popped up," he answered. "Secondly, that's also when her car was registered and she moved into an apartment in Kilwin…" He slid his finger across the screen. Jazz pulled it off the glass as if she'd done it countless times in their partnership. It didn't stop Declan's brother from continuing his explanation. "All within the span of a week. Before that there seems to be no trace of her. At least not on the internet or through the databases we have access to."

"But just because she isn't showing up on either doesn't mean Lydia didn't exist before then." Declan had to be the devil's advocate. Caleb looked up. His eyes were just as blue as Madi's and Des's.

"And yet you still think something's off with her," Caleb guessed.

Declan eyed the desks around them. A few deputies were in, their heads bent over paperwork. There wasn't any use in lying to his brother. Or Jazz, for that matter. They both were sharp as tacks when it came to reading someone. Even sharper when it came to their family and friends.

"I think Cooper Mann is telling the truth," he admitted. "I think Lydia either initiated the attack or carried it out against herself."

Caleb cringed. Jazz's sour expression wasn't too far off.

"Victim blaming is an absolute nonstarter, you know that, right?" Caleb pointed out. Declan didn't need the no-brainer statement. But, in this instance, his gut was starting to kick up a fuss.

Declan lowered his voice, leaning in so only they could hear him for sure.

"Which is why I want to be certain we check her out. If I'm wrong, then we've helped her case by shutting down any opposing argument Cooper's lawyer could put up in court. And if I'm right?" He shook his head. "Then we might start getting some answers around here. Some answers we desperately need."

Caleb kept his stare for a moment before sharing a look with Jazz. Declan remembered the first case they'd worked together as partners. Oil and water. Now? They could communicate in looks alone if they had to.

The look they shared must have been an agreement. Both nodded.

"So what do you want to do?" Caleb asked. "Want us to go talk to her?"

"What's her last known address? She said she lived in Overlook when we spoke in the hospital."

Jazz went back into the computer. It wasn't long before she had an answer. All three recognized the location. They'd passed that house countless times in the last year or so since Desmond's wife, Riley, used to live in the neighborhood with her twin and her son. Jenna and Hartley still resided in the house but Lydia's address, if memory served, was more toward the front of Willows Way.

Declan had to remind himself that just because he'd grown up in Overlook didn't mean he knew everyone who lived there, especially those who weren't long-time locals.

"Okay, let's divide and conquer on this." Declan

looked at Jazz. "Keep digging here and see if you can find her employer. If you do, give them a call and feel them out about her. Caleb, I want you to go to Cooper's house." Declan pulled a key out of his pocket. That earned a questioning look from both detectives. "Cooper gave me permission. He lives alone and in an apartment over where Delores stays. The number is on the key." He tossed him the key. Caleb caught it with ease. "See if you can't find something that helps us see if he's innocent or if he's playing us."

"And you?"

"I'll head over to Lydia's house to see if anything jumps out at me."

"I'm assuming you don't have a key to that one?"

"I don't."

Caleb and Jazz shared another look with each other and didn't comment out loud on whatever conclusion they'd reached. Instead, they all went about their tasks immediately.

Declan looked at his phone before jumping into Fiona.

No missed calls or texts from his chief deputy, Cussler. Which meant no news or leads on the two men and woman who had been a scourge against Main Street.

That should have concerned him more than the other nagging thought prickling at the back of his mind.

There were also no missed calls or texts from Remi.

He'd gone years without any contact whatsoever.

Yet, there he was. Thinking about her. Wondering what she was doing now. Craving more contact.

He knew her car was gone from his house and she was probably back at Heartland. Usually knowing that much would have been enough. Now he found his thoughts circling the woman.

Declan pulled her number up on his phone. He nearly called it right then and there. Then he tossed the cell onto the seat next to him and started toward the neighborhood of Willows Way.

The best thing he could do was rein in the chaos and sift through it until he could make his home, his county and the people within it safe.

If he couldn't do that?

Then what good could he ever be for his child?

Chapter Fourteen

The house was nice. One story. Brick. A ranch-style. There was a small front porch and a welcome mat on the concrete. The gardens on either side of it were well-kept, as were the yard and exterior of the house.

The neighbors were more than a stone's throw away, and no one appeared to be home in at least three of the houses.

It looked like a normal scene. A single woman who lived alone in a nice house in a nice neighborhood in a nice town.

Yet, after Declan knocked on the front door several times, he couldn't stop his gut from being loud again.

He'd met liars. He'd met scum.

He'd dealt with con artists, thieves, killers and men and women who wanted to watch the world burn.

He knew clever people who had lit the metaphorical or—on occasion—real match and the hapless idiots who believed they needed to be the ones to put that flame right where it needed to go.

Declan had met a lot of people, and only after a career of meeting those people did he think he was a good enough judge of character. Still, he knew he could be wrong. No man, woman or child could escape that human flaw.

Being wrong was what made being right feel so good.

It gave you a goal.

It gave you a purpose.

It made Declan know, logically, that he might be wrong about Cooper Mann.

The only thing that stopped that thought from really taking root was another fact he knew to be true.

Cooper Mann wasn't that smart.

As his mother would say, bless his heart, but Cooper wasn't burdened with an abundance of common sense.

There was no way that that boy could try to fool someone into believing he hadn't done what he had.

No, what had Declan believing him had to do with something he'd seen. Or, really, hadn't.

Cooper wasn't trying to hide a single thing.

He was just trying to get someone to believe him.

He wasn't clever enough to do anything else.

Declan didn't get back into his truck when no one answered the door. He moved to the living room windows and peered inside. The wooden slats of the blinds were open and through them he could see a standard living room setup. Couches, a TV, art on the wall, and a pair of tennis shoes next to the coffee table.

Declan kept moving. He left the front porch and rounded the side of the house next to the driveway. The house was flush with the ground and gave him easy access to look into each of the rooms along the exterior wall.

Easy access to *try* to look into each of the rooms.

Blinds were closed tightly over each window. The other side of the house was the same. Declan doubled back to the back porch. There were no blinds over the only window. He looked through it to a small, tidy kitchen.

Then he did something he shouldn't have.

He tried the back door.

When the knob turned without resistance, he expanded on what he shouldn't have been doing.

There were no beeps of an alarm or gasps of surprised houseguests. There was also no heat or airconditioning. The smell of disuse was as prevalent as the chill. Although Declan didn't believe anyone was in the house, still his hand went to the butt of the service weapon at his hip. He moved past the kitchen and took the first right he could, gut as quiet as the silence around him. He opened the first door he came to.

Then he moved to the next closed door and opened it. He went across the house to the last bedroom. And, just to be thorough, he checked the bathroom and moved to the kitchen and peeked at cupboards and drawers.

Declan cussed. Loud and true.

Empty.

The bedrooms, the bathroom, the kitchen.

He didn't know what was going on, but Declan would bet his badge that no one lived in the house.

Which meant Lydia had lied.

THE BARN WASN'T cold. Remi assumed they'd had the heaters running early that morning and the closed doors had kept in the warmth for the horses. There were two of them in the stables. Diamond Duke, a bay-and-white tobiano-patterned Tennessee walker who belonged to Josh, and Raphael, a chestnut Tennessee walker who belonged to Jonah.

Remi didn't know them like she had her horse, Jackson, growing up, but seeing the beautiful horses in their stalls made her feel better. For a moment it was just like any other normal day on Heartland.

Just as the thought took root, it was torn away from her.

A hand slapped around Remi's mouth as someone grabbed her arm.

Her grip had tightened around the revolver, ready to listen to her father's directive, when Jonah's voice floated next to her ear.

"One of them is around here somewhere," he whispered. "Keep quiet."

He moved his hand and, once again, Remi was led from out in the open to somewhere more hidden. This time instead of a bedroom, Jonah led her into Diamond Duke's stall. The horse watched with little interest as they came inside and closed the door behind them. Then again, his favorite human was leaning against him, hand running over his pristine coat.

Relief at seeing that Josh and Jonah were unhurt was, once again, short-lived.

"Are you okay?" Jonah asked, turning her enough to

look her up and down. His eyes widened at the blood. Their father's blood.

She nodded. Josh met her eye.

Jonah touched the blood on her shirt, looking for a wound. When he didn't find it he came to the same conclusion their brother already had. She could see it in both of their faces. Still, Josh voiced the question.

"Where's Dad?"

Remi knew this was the moment that could change everything. This was the moment she could do one of two things. She could let the unknown and the sorrow and the blood soaking through her father's shirt consume her. She could break down right then and there and let her brothers take over. Give them the gun, let them show her how they were both capable adults now and could handle themselves.

Or, she could woman up. Keep her father's promise and, instead of leaving Jonah and Josh to figure out how to get them all to safety, she could help. Show them that leaving the ranch didn't mean she'd retired the cowgirl.

"He made me leave him," she answered, no waver in her voice. It hardened like water being thrown into the freezing wind.

"He made you—" Josh started to repeat.

Remi didn't have time for it.

"He made me promise that we'd stay safe and that's what we're going to do," she steamrollered ahead. Remi looked to Jonah. Pain pinched his expression, though she knew it had nothing to do with anything physical. "Did you use the landline and call for help?"

He nodded, but then a different emotion momentarily took over his face.

"It didn't work. Not even a dial tone."

"And I'm assuming neither one of you have your cell phones."

It wasn't a question. Whereas most people around their ages were glued to their smartphones, Josh and Jonah were much like their father. There was no reason to have a phone out with the horses or while doing chores. Their father had preached that until it became second nature to *not* take their phones out of the house unless they were going to town. Even then Remi knew the chance of leaving the phones at the house was still great. The only reason she had bucked the anti-phone sentiment was because she'd stopped living on the ranch. Worrying about dropping her phone in horse droppings or having it crushed by a tractor hadn't been an issue in college or Nashville. Definitely not at her job as an accountant.

Which made the fact that the one time she actually *needed* it and didn't have it that much more frustrating.

"They're in the living room," Jonah answered. "Once the shooting started we had to bolt back into the kitchen and then out the back door."

"You said there's someone around here?" she asked, her mind building up a new plan.

"Right after we got in here we saw two men walking the backyard." Josh eyed the revolver in her hand. "They had guns."

"Two men were upstairs. Dad told me not to shoot

if there was more than one. So five against three, including Lydia."

Jonah flinched at the name.

"Why is this even happening? Why is *she* here? Did I do this somehow? Is she here because of me? I don't understand!"

"Me." Her brothers' eyebrows rose in tandem. "Before Lydia attacked she said she was here for me."

"But why?" The question was barely out of Josh's mouth before Jonah's eyes widened even more. He looked at Remi, and she knew he'd stumbled onto the same theory she'd already been working on in the back of her mind.

One that made her stomach drop and blood boil at the same time.

"Is it because you're pregnant with the sheriff's baby?" Jonah asked. "She could have heard you tell me in the hospital."

"It's a long-shot guess but that's all I can figure. He's the only one of us who does anything that might catch this kind of heat."

"Wait, you're pregnant?"

Remi turned to Josh and nodded. She felt bad he was finding out like this but, as was the current story of her life, she just didn't have the time to address the topic with loving care.

The best she could do was give him a brief, apologetic smile.

Then it was down to business.

"Which is another reason we're about to get the hell out of here." Remi motioned to the gun, careful to keep its aim away from the three of them and Diamond Duke. "From what I remember this has eight rounds. I'm going to go ahead and assume our five bad guys all have guns, all have more bullets, and all know how to use them better than us." She waited a beat for her brothers to interject. They didn't. "So, since we haven't been able to call for help, standing our ground in here with eight bullets that aren't even guaranteed to hit their target sounds like an awful plan."

Remi looked to the stall across the aisle from them.

Raphael, ever content, let out a little neigh.

"Which is why we're going to focus on being the best cowboys we can be."

"You want us to ride out," Jonah said.

Remi nodded.

"Our best option is to put distance between us and them. Ride to the Nash Ranch and hope somebody's home."

"That's a long ride out in the open," Jonah pointed out. "Once we clear the last barn on Heartland that's easy pickings in the fields between us and them. What… maybe ten minutes or so."

Josh motioned around them.

"I'd rather be the fish in the pool than fish in the barrel." He put his hand on Remi's shoulder and nodded. His support rallied her even more.

"I'll unlatch the back doors. Y'all tack up your horses like our lives depend on it." Which they did.

"There's no doubles saddle in here. Going to be a bumpy ride for you," Josh said.

"Better than being those fish."

They got to work quickly. Remi went back to the door she'd come through and barred it, checked the main double doors to make sure they were still locked, and then hurried to the back two. They were usually only opened to take advantage of cool air and breezes for the horses. Now they were all that stood between her relative calm and all-out fear.

Remi checked that the doors were still locked. She undid the latch slowly, careful not to make a sound, but didn't open them.

Not yet.

She didn't know where any of the men or Lydia were. They could be in the house still or the area around the barn, or they could simply have left. The fact that she had no idea was terrifying.

How long ago had she run from her father's side? Five minutes ago? Ten? Maybe more?

If they were still on the ranch, Remi had to believe they'd check the closest building to the house. Sooner rather than later.

It put her nerves closer to the edge and sent pricks of adrenaline across her body. Her muscles tightened in anticipation. Her palms grew sweaty. Remi strained to listen past her brothers tacking up their horses in record time.

Then she heard something she'd prayed she wouldn't.

A feeling of dread rolled over in her stomach. The hairs on the back of her neck stood on end.

The door they'd all come in through might have been locked but someone jiggling the handle was like a gun-shot in the silence. Remi hurried to the space between the horse stalls her brothers were in. Both had paused what they were doing.

"Keep going," she whispered.

Someone coming to the barn didn't change their plan. There was nowhere to hide, and their odds of five against one gun was still not something she wanted to test.

She stood there and listened.

The door was at the head of the barn, off to the left. Stalls blocked her view of it. If someone broke through she'd have a few seconds to react. Whether that was jumping on a horse or shooting.

"Done."

Remi could have sung in relief as her brothers whispered in unison. Josh opened his stall's door. Remi went to Jonah's.

Whoever was on the other side of the barn door decided they were done trying things the normal way. The *bang* of someone ramming the door made Diamond Duke do a little jump as Josh led him into the aisle. He waved Raphael through but didn't follow as he and Jonah went to the door. Remi held back, too, and together they heard another loud bang followed by the splintering of wood.

They'd run out of time.

There was no way all three of them could mount up and ride out now. Not without being targets.

What would Declan do?

The question popped into Remi's head so quickly she answered it before she thought of why she'd asked it in the first place.

She took a small step forward so that she was in front of her little brother and raised the revolver.

She wasn't going to let anyone hurt any more of her family.

Not today.

Not ever.

Chapter Fifteen

The moment he saw her, Declan thought he was dreaming.

Honest to God, he thought he'd somehow fallen asleep somewhere between Lydia's house, Winding Road and his mother's house.

He wasn't even supposed to *be* on his way to the main house on the Nash Family Ranch. After he'd discovered Lydia's place was empty, he'd called Caleb to tell him the news. Caleb thought that was wildly peculiar but hadn't been able to make it to Cooper's place yet to see if there were any more wildly peculiar finds. Instead, he'd said he was almost to their ranch.

"Cooper Mann's family must have some crazy Spidey senses," he'd said. "Ma just called and said his grandma June is sitting at her dining table, wanting to talk to us."

"Why didn't she go to the department or call us?"

Caleb had snorted.

"Southern women are most powerful when they have a glass of sweet tea in front of them and some kind of wicker chair beneath them. But seriously, if you had to talk to the law, wouldn't you rather do it while basking in Mom's hospitality?"

Declan had seen the logic in that. Plus, there was probably some way their mother knew June Mann through everything she did in the community. Which meant telling the older woman to go to the department was a no-no. Not unless they wanted to catch their mother's wrath.

So Declan had decided to meet his brother and Grandma June at the ranch. On the drive there he'd percolated the information he did and didn't have and had almost tuned so wholly into his own thoughts that he didn't clock the movement streaking across the field he was driving alongside.

If seeing Remi galloping through an open field, hair blowing in the wind behind her wasn't a dream then maybe it was fate.

Because Declan didn't have to know the circumstances around why she was booking it for him to know exactly where she was going.

The same place he was.

Declan might have spent a bit more time speculating dreams and fate and Lydia's empty home and Grandma June's unannounced arrival if the other shocking details hadn't filtered through.

Remi wasn't alone.

Her brother, Jonah judging by his height, was trailing behind her on another horse. While someone was pressed against Remi's chest. The man was slumped, head bent.

Something was wrong.

Something was horribly wrong.

Declan honked the horn, unlocked his phone and dialed the last number on his recent calls list. The second it rang he put it on speaker and then cut his wheel.

The Nash Family Ranch and Hudson Heartland both had fenced in most of their acreage. However, after a dispute that came before any of the children of either family were born, there was a stretch of land between them that neither believed the other should claim. A no-man's-land, his father had called it. Owned and not owned by two families. Their only agreement concerning the expanse was that neither could erect a fence or let livestock or horses roam there.

Declan had never cared about the space.

Until now.

Caleb answered the phone just as Declan navigated the slight dip of the road's shoulder and began driving out into the field. He honked the horn again. This time Remi turned her head to look.

She must have yelled something to Jonah. Both slowed.

"What's going on?" Caleb asked.

"Remi and Jonah are booking it on horses to the ranch through no-man's-land. Remi's carrying someone who looks hurt."

Rustling carried through the airwaves. Caleb was moving.

"How hurt we talking?"

Declan was eating up the distance between them and came to a stop a few yards off, not wanting to spook the horses.

He swore as Remi and Jonah trotted over.

"She's holding Josh and there's blood all over both of them."

Declan threw open the door, adrenaline shooting through him so fast that he thought it might make him explode. Josh was pressed against Remi's front, and he could see blood across her arm and the hand holding the reins.

And the gun she had clutched in the hand pressing Josh against her.

"Lydia Cartwright and at least four men are on the ranch," Remi dived in, panting. "Dad's upstairs in the house with a bullet in the stomach. Josh just got hit in the chest. They need a hospital. *Now.*"

Declan put his phone between his shoulder and his ear.

"You get that?"

"Yeah," Caleb answered. "Calling for EMS and backup."

Jonah swung off his horse and Declan motioned to Josh. He was unconscious. Remi's expression was blank.

"Let's get Josh in the truck," he said. "Hold on, Caleb."

He dropped his phone into his front breast pocket and, together with Jonah, pulled Josh down from the horse. Remi stayed astride while the two of them slid Josh into the passenger seat.

Then Declan only had eyes for Remi.

If the blood on her arm and hand had been alarming, the blood on front of her shirt was downright heart-stopping. She caught his eye.

"It's my dad's, not mine."

Declan knew that shouldn't have made him feel better.

It did.

He pulled his phone back out.

"Caleb, call ahead to the ER and say we have Josh Hudson with a gunshot wound to the chest coming in hot with Jonah and Remi in my truck."

Jonah didn't need any prodding. He looped around the truck to the open driver's side door. Declan held his hand up to Remi to help her down.

She wasn't having it. Her grip on the reins tightened.

Declan was reminded of the girl whose father used to tame wild horses. The one who could outride him and his siblings even if they'd never admit it. The girl who had grown up more cowgirl than he had cowboy, if he was being honest.

"You're going back to the house. So am I."

Remi straightened her shoulders.

Declan, Jonah and even Caleb spoke at once.

She didn't listen.

"I left Dad for my kid's sake. I'm going back for him for the same reason." She pulled the reins to the side, turning her horse around and effectively ending the discussion. She turned to Jonah. "Go. Now." Then she gave Declan a long, low look. "I can outride you and you know it. Telling me I can't go only wastes time we don't have."

What Declan felt at her statements of fact was jarring. On the one hand he wanted to cuff her and throw her into the truck, sending her off to safety, kicking and screaming if need be. On the other hand, he'd never been more proud.

Remi Hudson was a fighter.

So was he.

And they'd both be damned if their kid didn't get the chance to be, too.

Declan nodded to Jonah and then went to his horse.

"Caleb," he said, "Remi and I will be approaching from no-man's-land."

"Des is here so I'm bringing him with me. Be safe, keep your phone on and in your pocket."

"Roger that."

Remi and her family might have been near-professionals when it came to horseback riding, but that didn't mean Declan was an amateur. The second he was upright in the saddle and fingers laced around the reins, he felt something like what he thought a professional swimmer might feel when first diving into the lap pool. Adrenaline, natural and exciting, flooded his veins, tensing his muscles and making his heart gallop. Being on a horse was being at home.

He knew Remi felt the same.

In tandem they struck out back toward Heartland. Thundering across the field like a battle cry. Hooves against the earth. Cold air biting at their faces. Furious justice at their heels.

Two horses and their riders in sync.

It felt right, even if the reason they were riding was so wrong.

Declan glanced over at the woman next to him and knew without a doubt that he'd never find another person like her ever again.

Remi Hudson was one of a kind.

And he loved her for it.

Declan slowed as the barn nearest the house came into view. Thankfully, so did Remi. Although her bravado was still displayed fiercely across her face, he saw caution there, too. She'd come back for her father but wasn't about to put their child at unnecessary risk. At least, no more than coming back had.

"For us to get out on the horses I had to shoot one of them," she said with effort. Her cheeks were red with windburn and exertion. Being pregnant probably wasn't helping. He remembered how tired Madi and Nina had been during the beginnings of their pregnancies.

"Did you kill him?" he had to ask.

The question didn't even make her flinch.

"I thought I did but he shot Josh before I could make sure. We barely got him on the horse before another one of them ran into the barn. We took off, but no one shot at us again."

Declan nodded, hoping that one man was out of commission by now.

"Stay behind me," he said. "If anyone shoots at us, use me and the horses as cover if you have to."

Declan took the lead, trotting ahead with eyes peeled and gun in one hand.

No one moved.

He led them to the side of the barn facing away from the house and jumped off his horse. Remi followed suit.

She hung back as he moved around the corner to look inside the barn.

Blood was in the aisle between the stalls. Two spots of them on opposite ends. There was no one inside to match them.

"The barn nearest the house is empty," he said down to his pocket so Caleb could hear through the speakerphone that was still on. Caleb said he understood.

"Des and I are coming up the drive now."

Declan could feel Remi's anxiety mounting as he peered around what used to be a door, splintered off the hinges and facing the house.

"No movement."

Caleb repeated the sentiment when they made it to the end of the driveway opposite them.

"Let's clear the house," Declan ordered. "Be careful."

Remi stuck to Declan's back as they moved to the house in a hurry. For the next few minutes the four of them went from room to room, only to clarify it was empty.

The men and Lydia were gone.

And the only things they'd left behind were blood and Gale Hudson.

Sirens blared up the driveway when they finally made it to the upstairs bathroom the Hudson patriarch was in.

It wasn't a pretty sight.

Remi cried out, pure anguish breaking down every part of the woman. She reached out for her father before she'd even cleared the doorway. Declan grabbed her, trying to shield her from a terrifying reality if only for a few seconds longer.

Even if he didn't know what had happened in the bathroom, it was clear that Gale had fought. Blood was smeared everywhere, the man himself in the middle of it all and as still as still could be.

Remi fought against Declan's chest.

Desmond ran past them and knelt beside Gale. He checked his pulse.

He didn't shake his head, but he didn't look relieved, either.

UNLIKE THE LAST time chaos had reigned within their orbit, Declan didn't leave Remi's side once.

From Heartland to the hospital to roaming the halls of the hospital to even standing outside of the bathroom door, the sheriff kept his cowboy hat on but metaphorically seemed to take his badge off.

"Go do what you need to," Remi had said after Josh had first gone into surgery. Declan had shaken his head. She'd noticed for the first time that day that dark stubble was lining his chin.

"I'm with you now," was all he'd said in response.

These were words that were comforting in an increasingly uncertain world, and words he stayed true to.

He made and answered phone calls, spoke to his brothers, deputies and chief deputy in person, and when it was time for her to relay everything that had happened at Heartland, he was the one who took her statement personally.

Remi had been ready to ride solo back to the ranch

to try to save her dad but now she was grateful for the close proximity. Especially when, hours later, Jonah met them next to a vending machine in the lobby.

He ran a hand through his hair. He was exhausted.

"I just talked to the doctor about Dad."

Remi perked up at that. She'd been hovering around the hallways in the hopes of talking to a doctor sometime soon. Her father was still alive, a miracle by all accounts, and had gone through a series of touch-and-go surgeries. He'd only been sent to a room an hour ago. Josh, who had undergone his own surgery, had been out for four. He'd regained consciousness only to ask about them and then the "new fling" Jonah had told Remi about.

After a deputy had found and brought their phones to the hospital, Remi had made sure to call the woman after she realized how important she was to her brother. They had all been surprised when a brightly dressed, extremely expressive woman named Lilianna had rushed into the hospital and immediately to his bedside. Talking to the woman, seeing how worried she was, had eased Remi's guilt at leaving Josh's side.

It had given her more time to worry about their father.

"How is he?" Remi asked, heart jumping back into her throat. "Does he have to have another surgery?"

Jonah shook his head. Then he did something she'd truly not seen coming. He smiled.

"His rehab is going to be extensive and he'll have to take it easy for a long while to come, *but* the doc said he should be out of the woods now. He's stable and both

surgeries did exactly what they wanted them to do."
Remi threw her arms around her brother in an embrace.
He spoke into her hair. "If you hadn't gotten him help
as fast as you did, it would be a different story."

Remi squeezed and then pulled away. She looked
him in the eye with certainty.

"And if you hadn't gotten Josh here as fast as you
did, *he* would have been in worse trouble, too."

Jonah took the truth with a smile that waned.

"But if I'd never gone out with Lydia—" he started.

"They would have still probably come," Declan finished.

They'd already had this conversation while waiting
for Josh and their dad's surgeries to finish. Jonah told
Declan and Caleb everything he knew about Lydia,
which hadn't been much. She'd been nice and funny
and had done a good job at pulling Jonah in with lim-
ited interaction.

The truth was, no one blamed him one bit, yet Remi
could see he'd be blaming himself for a long while despite that fact.

Jonah shook himself a little.

"Did you talk to Mom?"

"Yeah. Her flight got grounded because of the
weather and it took all I had to convince her and Dave
not to drive through it instead. She only relented after
hearing that Josh and Dad would be okay. She'll call
one of us tomorrow with an update but said *you* better
call her soon."

Jonah glanced at Declan. He lowered his voice.

"Does she know? About the…you know?"

Remi felt Declan's gaze switch to her. She shook her head.

"I want to tell her in person."

"She'd like that." Jonah let out a loud, long sigh. "What she *wouldn't* like is you running yourself into the ground while pregnant with her only claim to a grand-kid." He fixed her with a mock stern expression. "Get out of here and get some rest."

Remi opened her mouth to complain, but he cut her off.

"I called Rick, Dad's friend, and he said he wants to come up here and stay the night with Dad while I stay with Josh. There's no reason you need to stay here, too." He looked to Declan. "I'm assuming Remi has a place to stay with you, though?"

"She does."

"But what if—" Remi tried.

Jonah still wasn't having it.

"But what if nothing. I'll let you know if *anything* happens. Plus, it's not like the ranch is that far from here anyways." He put his hands on her shoulders to focus her attention so that it stayed solely on him and his next words. "You shot a man to get us off the ranch and then went right back to it to get Dad. Let me do this very simple task of watching over everyone here." His expression softened. "Give me this, Remi. I need it."

So, she did.

Then, before she knew it, Remi was standing in Declan's bathroom back on the Nash Family Ranch and staring at a mirror that was starting to steam over from the shower heating up behind her. She'd already stripped naked but couldn't get her feet to move from the tile floor.

All because of the stain on her skin.

Blood from her father or her brother that had seeped through her shirt.

Remi knew they were okay now, but that crimson smear held too much power still.

Way too much.

It wasn't until two beautiful green eyes met her gaze head-on that Remi realized she was sobbing.

And it wasn't until Declan's arms wrapped around her naked body that she realized how much she needed the man.

Chapter Sixteen

Sometime in the dark of late night or early morning, Remi woke up in bed alone. It wasn't her bed, and she sussed that out pretty quickly through the haze of sleep thanks to the way the pillow smelled beneath her still-wet hair.

It smelled like spice and the woods and Declan Nash.

Remi rolled over and felt the empty space next to her.

After her breakdown in the bathroom, Declan had gone above and beyond the call of supportive. Not only had he taken her into the shower with his jeans still on, he'd scrubbed the blood off her skin and held her while she cried some more. Only after she'd regained her composure, or enough of it to stop crying, did the man dry her off, put a too-big shirt over her head and deposit her like a child in bed.

Remi had been so exhausted from her outburst to the adrenaline-filled day she'd had that sleep had overtaken her within the space of two blinks.

Now she guessed that the man who had saved her from herself hadn't gotten beneath those same sheets next to her.

Remi rolled back over and found her phone on the nightstand. No new calls or texts from Jonah. She took that as good news and slowly got out of bed. She flushed when she realized she was wearing a pair of boxers. She didn't remember putting those on.

Declan surely was a caring and sly man.

If he hadn't already seen her as naked as naked could be, she might have been so embarrassed that she'd try to escape. Instead, she opened the door between the bedroom and living room with all the hope in the world of seeing the sheriff.

She wasn't disappointed.

Declan looked up from his laptop on the coffee table with alarm. That alarm softened after a moment. He smiled.

"Hey, Huds."

It was such a simple greeting, yet it shifted something inside of her that had already been moving.

"Hey, Sheriff."

Remi settled in the chair kitty-corner to the couch so she could face him the best she could.

"Thank you for earlier, by the way. I kind of *lost it*, lost it."

Declan waved off the apology.

"I only did what I could do to help." He sighed and glanced at the computer. "I just wish I could do more."

"I take that to mean no one has found Lydia and the men?"

He ran a hand over the stubble along his jaw. Whatever had softened his expression was now gone. Stress and frustration took its place.

"No. We've checked all the hospitals in the county, and even reached out past it, to see if we can't locate the guy you got. We have so many APBs out on them *and* the three who pulled what they pulled on Main Street that the gossip mill is about to shatter. Mom said that Cooper Mann's grandmother let her know in no uncertain terms that Overlook is losing faith in the department. In me. And, honestly, I can't blame them." He dragged his gaze to hers. "We have so many weird little pieces to this chaotic puzzle, and I just can't seem to find a way to force them to fit. For a moment I'll think I have something and then it gets lost in the chaos. It's driving me crazy."

Remi didn't say anything right away. She knew the man well enough that telling him everything was going to be okay, telling him that he *would* get all of the bad guys in the end, wasn't actually going to help him.

So, instead, she told him a story.

"One time when I was younger Dad and I went to a ranch out in Texas to visit a friend of his named Barry. The boys were too young and Mom had to stay to watch them and, to be honest, I wasn't that excited to be the one who had to go. Dad knew it and tried to talk the place up before we even got there. He told me it was three times bigger than Heartland and had all kinds of animals everywhere you looked. I didn't believe him— to me Heartland was massive—but then we drove the road to the main house and it felt like it took a lifetime to get there. All along the way I watched herds of cows grazing, people horseback riding, and even saw some goats running around. I was mesmerized." Remi couldn't help the smile that she knew passed over her face. The little-kid awe she'd felt then was hard to forget even as an adult. "So when Barry invited us to move the herd of cows to a field at the opposite end of his property, I was actually excited. We got our own horses, our own tents, and some stuff to make s'mores, and rode all day until we got them to where they needed to be. That night I passed out with chocolate on my mouth and a sore butt from riding. It was magic."

Declan smiled in turn at that.

"Later that night, though, I woke up to the sound of two hundred scared cattle. I'd barely gotten on my horse before they took off in all different directions," she continued. "I couldn't figure out what was going on, and neither could Dad or the ranch hands who had come with us. There was too much noise, too much movement, and not enough light. And do you know what Barry did?"

Declan raised his eyebrow in question. Remi leaned forward in her seat.

"He took a breath, tuned the world out and reminded himself that he'd been a rancher for years and was damn good at it. *That's* when he spotted the wolf."

Remi moved from her seat to the spot next to Declan and put her hand on his knee. She wanted to encourage him and comfort him all at the same time. She hoped that she'd at least hit one of her targets.

Declan angled his body so he could meet her gaze more easily.

Once again Remi marveled at how different this

scene would have been if they were younger. *He* would have been the one talking while *she* listened in silence.

"With what I know from growing up in Overlook and from what I've heard since I've been gone, chaos seems to be more frequent than not. You've lived in it and still live in it. You're *good* at navigating it. Now you just need to take a breath, tune the world out, and trust that you're—"

Calling him *fast* was an injustice to the move he actually pulled off. In one fluid movement Declan went from a statue beneath her hand to heat against her lips.

He cupped the side of her face and Remi leaned in to the surprise.

She kissed the man back.

Hard.

Their lips parted and the taste of him was all she wanted in the world.

When he broke the kiss, Remi was left blinking and confused.

"You," he rasped out.

"Me?"

"You," he repeated. "That's what I want."

He was back to her lips within the space of a breath. The wild boy from her childhood and teen years. The reunited friend. The good—and not mention to last—fling. The accidental father of her child. The sheriff savior.

Declan Nash had a list of ever-evolving meanings to her.

But what was he now? Between a night of passion

that wasn't supposed to last through the next day to always being connected through their unborn child.

What would happen next?

Coparenting across state lines due to her promotion?

Getting married in no-man's-land while her belly grew?

Or some form of in-between?

Remi had no idea about their future.

But she did know something about the present.

She looped her arms around Declan's neck and pulled him against her until they were lying across the couch. He followed her down while never breaking their kiss. In fact, he deepened it with his tongue, trapping a moan of pleasure between them.

Declan's hand tangled in her hair while the other gripped her hip. She moved up and against him as he tried to maneuver himself so his body weight wasn't solely on her. In the process Remi felt how much Declan Nash truly wanted her.

It put fire straight through her. She dropped her hands down and went for the hem of his shirt. Remi had never wanted something gone as badly as she wanted that shirt off.

Declan felt her frustration. He broke their kiss and nearly ripped it in two. The shirt went flying and then he was focused on hers. Which was *also* his. A fact that must have encouraged him. He grabbed its hem and then tore it right up the middle.

Cold air hit Remi's bare chest as the two sides of the fabric fell away, but there were only flames in her blood. When he dropped his mouth down to the skin of her neck and then followed a tantalizing path to her nipple, Remi almost cussed him.

When his hardness pushed against the boxers she was somehow still wearing and through the shorts *he* was somehow still wearing, Remi nearly lost it.

The second he came up for air, she decided to end the torture.

She pulled him back down on top of her and moaned.

It seemed to do the trick.

Remi moved against him as, one-handed, he took off his shorts. Then he focused on her. She moaned again as his hand, strong and warm, skimmed down the boxers on loan and then came back up her leg. Trailing heat and lust right to the spot where she wanted his attention next.

There was no trapping her moans now.

She yelled out in absolute bliss as he pushed inside of her and filled her with hard passion. She moved against him with uncontainable desire.

A man and a woman desperate to be closer.

Lips to lips.

Skin to skin.

Galloping heartbeats.

Remi didn't know what their future held but she did know one thing.

She wanted Declan, too.

THE PHONE CALL didn't wake Declan, Remi did.

Tangled together between the sheets of his bed, she couldn't help thrashing around to escape to the bathroom.

Declan immediately went on high alert, fighting through the haze of the good sleep he'd fallen into with the naked woman wrapped in his arms. He followed her up and out of the bed, fists balled and eyes wild. It didn't matter that he was as naked as the day he was born, he was going to fight tooth and nail to combat whatever had woken Remi so violently.

Then he heard her in the bathroom heaving.

There wasn't anything he could punch or shoot to cure morning sickness.

So after Remi shooed him away, Declan went to the kitchen and poured her a glass of water and took stock of what he had to eat. Nina, Caleb's wife, had claimed that sour candy had been a lifesaver when she'd first been pregnant with their son. Madi hadn't really felt sick with Addison but with her second pregnancy she'd always had crackers, some kind of Popsicle, and a lot of snacks. Declan hadn't been grocery shopping in a hot minute. All he had that met the criteria was a bag of pretzels Desmond had left the week before.

They would have to do.

He plated some, set the water next to it, and brought his phone back out to him.

That was when he saw the missed call. It was from Cussler and time-stamped at just after three in the morning. It was now almost five.

There were no texts or emails as a follow-up. No voice mail, either.

Declan wondered if it had been an accident. His chief deputy was a married man and a father to four. Declan only liked to call him when it was absolutely necessary.

He decided to send a text, instead. He put the phone down and the ringer up, surprised he'd missed the call in the first place. Normally he was a light sleeper. Then again, normally, he didn't have a naked Remi Hudson in his bed.

No sooner had he set the phone down than the woman of the hour made her entrance. She was wearing another one of his old T-shirts. It was too big for her and somehow still she made it an attractive piece. The urge to rip it off her like he'd done earlier was nearly overpowering. She frowned at him, picking up on his thoughts.

"Don't go getting any ideas, buddy. I feel like death incarnate. I know it's cliché to blame you for how I feel right now, but—" she took a seat at the dining table next to him "—this is all your fault."

Declan chuckled.

"The words every man wants to hear after a night of rolling around naked in bed with a beautiful woman."

That pulled a smile from her. It was small but there. She motioned to the plate of pretzels. He nodded.

"I didn't know if you would want to eat but read that if you eat a little every few hours that it might help with morning sickness, especially when you first wake up."

Remi's eyebrow arched high.

He unlocked his phone and found the app he was looking for. He tapped it and slid the phone over.

The surprise was clear on her face.

"You downloaded a pregnancy app?"

Declan shrugged.

"I figure I'm already behind on the game, might as well try to catch up best I can."

Remi gave him a look he couldn't quite place and grabbed a handful of pretzels.

"If I didn't feel like I was about to be sick, starve, and cry all at the same time right now I'd kiss you."

Declan smirked.

"And if you kissed me right now I might just destroy another one of my shirts."

Remi's cheeks flushed pink and she laughed.

"Smooth one, Sheriff."

"I try."

The phone between them buzzed.

Remi tensed.

"I missed a call from my chief deputy. I texted him I was up," he explained, spinning the phone around to face him. "If something was wrong he would have called more than once or probably just come here to wake me up himself."

He trailed off when the phone started to ring. He stopped whatever he was going to say and took the call right there. Cussler was quick and precise. He'd called Declan, then decided to let the sheriff get some sleep when he hadn't answered. It was no secret Declan hadn't gotten enough of it lately. Cussler recounted what had happened and had handled the situation.

Declan thanked him and ordered him to seek the same sleep he'd let Declan get.

As they ended their call, Declan was already slipping deep into his thoughts.

Finally Remi said, "What's wrong? What happened?"

He didn't answer right away. If it had been yesterday afternoon the new information would have been another piece in the bizarre puzzle. Another stroke of chaos. Another reminder that he had no idea what *exactly* was going on.

But Declan had since had some sleep, some comfort, and a woman who'd told a story about a rancher and a wolf.

Now he finally saw some sense in the chaos.

Declan met Remi's gaze. She had a pretzel at her lips and was undoubtedly the most stunning woman he'd ever seen.

"I think it's time I called a family meeting."

Chapter Seventeen

The last time Remi had been in the same room as all of the Nash siblings, they had been in the loft of their stable and hoping they wouldn't get caught by the adults they'd snuck away from. There had been others there, friends and crushes and hangers-on, because being a Nash in Overlook earned a certain amount of fame. Unwanted by them, given by most.

When the triplets were together, even more so.

Remi had never liked the attention thrust upon them. They clearly didn't want it. However, talking to each as they showed up at Declan's house, she was glad to see it hadn't beaten them down.

Like their older brother, the triplets were and were not the same as she remembered.

Outside of the sheriff's department, Caleb was smiles and humor. He had a coffee cup in one hand and a baby teething ring in the other. He declared to everyone that he'd found it in his truck and wasn't going to let it out of his sight until he could pass it to his wife, Nina, since it was one of their son's favorite things to play with. Love had drenched every word.

Madi, who been closed off to everyone who wasn't her family when they were younger, embraced Remi with a warm hug. The scar along her cheek was just as noticeable as it had always been, but it did nothing to dampen her lighthearted spirit. She plopped down on the couch next to Caleb and started to tell him about her two children's current favorite toys. One was the remote control to their TV. The other was a gardening bucket with a painted smiley face on it. Both laughed at that.

Desmond came in last. The limp he walked with hadn't changed from when they were younger but there was definitely something different about it and him. A lightness? A carefree air around him? Remi couldn't place her finger on it but accepted a hug from him with pleasure. He was a businessman who had spent his career helping others. He hadn't had to come with Caleb to Heartland the day before, but he had, no hesitation. Remi thanked him for it and he accepted the kind words with a charming Nash smile before moving into the living room to sit.

Then there they were.

The Nash triplets.

Once they had been three eight-year-olds forced to live through trauma no kid should have to experience.

Taken from a park during a game of hide-and-seek. Hurt, scared and terrified.

Now three adults, happy and healthy—and no idea they were about to revisit a past they'd all seemed to move on from.

Remi knew this same thought was moving through

Declan's mind the moment he came in from the bedroom and saw them. He shared a look with her.

She tried on an encouraging smile.

It wasn't missed.

Madi stopped whatever Caleb was saying to Desmond by putting her hands on both of their arms. They followed her gaze to Declan. The three of them looked up at their big brother as he pulled a chair from next to the dining table opposite them. He waited until Remi was sitting in the armchair before he started.

"I'm going to dive in because I've already held off telling any of you this for too long as it is." Still, Declan took a breath before continuing. The triplets lost their earlier humor. Three sets of baby blues were focused solely on him. "The morning before Cooper Mann allegedly attacked Lydia Cartwright he asked to meet me because he thought he had information on a cold case. *Your* cold case." The shift was subtle but there. The triplets tensed in unison. "He said a man in a fancy suit at the Waypoint Bar kept rattling on about a note in the wall at Well Water Cabin that law enforcement had missed. I thought it was a bunch of nonsense but, well, I had to check. Remi was in town and nice enough to indulge me with a fresh pair of eyes. Which made the difference because she found it."

"A note *in* the wall?" Caleb repeated.

Declan nodded.

"It looked like a painted-over wallpaper seam," Remi explained. "Basically it was glued against the wall in the paint. I almost didn't see it."

"What did it say?" Madi scooted to the edge of the

couch cushion. Her darkened expression reminded Remi of how she'd often looked as a teen.

Declan pulled out his phone, selected one of the pictures he'd taken of the note and passed it to her. They took turns looking at it even though Declan answered.

"Justin Redman was the only thing written on it."

"Why does that name sound familiar?" Desmond asked.

Caleb was quick to answer.

"Dad was on a case trying to find his attacker just before the abduction, right?"

Declan nodded.

"I took another look at the file last night to see if anything stuck out to me, but it was pretty cut-and-dried. Dad was about to go after his attacker hard and then had to let someone else handle the case after the abduction. Justin was killed in a car accident before another detective could take the case so it was ultimately dropped."

Madi scrolled through Declan's phone.

"I guess he got really lucky, then," she muttered. Then she amended, "The attacker. Not Justin, obviously. You know how good Dad was at cases like that."

They all nodded in agreement. Declan continued.

"Before I could really get a grasp of what we'd found, Cooper was arrested. I assumed he was pulling my leg with the note, painted it in there a while back and used it to distract me. Or it was a twisted way to drum up *more* publicity for himself after he tried to kidnap Lydia. You know how some of these bad guys love the spotlight."

Desmond snorted.

"It would have been a doozy of a news bulletin, too.

'A new lead following Overlook's most infamous kidnapping case found at the same time local idiot kidnaps, or tries to, an innocent woman.' If he did it for attention he'd surely get it."

"But you didn't go public with the note." Caleb's voice held an edge. He was angry he hadn't been told. Not only was he Declan's brother, he was one of his detectives.

"We had to handle the situation as delicately and quickly as we could, given the town's history," Declan defended. "I had to put the *maybe* of the abduction case on the back burner while I dealt with the very real and present attempted abduction. And all before the press tore into us to make that job harder."

Madi continued looking at Declan's phone. Desmond nodded. Caleb was satisfied enough not to argue.

"Cooper denied he attacked Lydia and said *she* attacked him, mutilated her face with his keys, and then jumped into his car. A witness saw him and assumed he was pushing her inside. He said he was trying to get her out while Lydia swore up and down that he attacked and was trying to take her when we interviewed her. I was going to dig deeper into Justin Redman, still, but the next day I got distracted again."

"Claire's Café?" Madi guessed.

What had happened across Main Street had already circulated twice over throughout the county.

"Yeah," Declan answered gruffly. "A man jumps out of a car outside, attacks a woman, and I give chase. Once he's standing still he tells me, in so many words, that he wanted me to chase him away from Claire's. I run back to find out a man and woman, both wearing suits, had come inside and shot a man in the arm before escaping back to their car. They then go and pick up the man I'd been chasing."

None of the triplets commented. Again, they knew this part.

Well, most of it.

They didn't know why Remi hadn't been shot and, somehow, the news hadn't made its way to them.

"And then we have yesterday," he continued. "I talked to Cooper on a hunch and became convinced he's not lying."

"Then Jazz and I figure out that Lydia Cartwright didn't exist, at least not online, until five years ago," Caleb supplied. "And you go to her house and find out it's empty, meaning she lied."

Remi hadn't known that part. She gave Declan a questioning look. He returned it with an apologetic one.

"I was heading to Heartland to talk to Jonah again. See if he knew anything about the house and why she'd lied. But changed course here when Cooper's grandma showed up to plead his case. I saw you in the field before I ever made it off Winding Road." He redirected his attention to his siblings to, she guessed, tell them about what had happened on Heartland before they'd met in the field. However, the words stuck in his mouth.

Declan became angry. A muscle in his jaw twitched. His hands fisted.

Remi spoke for him.

"My brothers, Dad and I were making some food when Lydia showed up. She said she had come for me, not Jonah, and immediately attacked. I was able to get her out of the house, but she opened fire." Remi felt her own bad memories tensing her body. She took a breath and skipped the heart-wrenching parts. "It wasn't until I made it out to the barn behind our house to where Jonah and Josh were that I found out there were four men with her, all armed. I shot one in the stomach before Josh was shot. After that we managed to ride off. My brothers said no one spoke to them or around them when they were trying to hide. If—if my dad heard anything, it might be a while before we can find out what that was."

Each Nash gave her a sympathetic look. She was thankful they didn't say anything. There wasn't much reassurance they could give her at the moment. Sometimes a look of understanding or a pat on the back helped more than words. A sentiment the family was, no doubt, well versed in by now.

"Which brings us to early this morning," Declan continued. "Cussler called this morning to tell me that a man named Joe Langley was taken to the ER early. He was attacked during a jog through his neighborhood after he couldn't sleep. He said a man in a suit came out of nowhere, did the deed, and left him with his phone to call for help."

"It seems like the Fixers are our common link between everything that's happened," Caleb jumped in. "We might not be able to see their scorpion tattoos but their suits *and* frustrating-as-hell ability to stay a few steps ahead of law enforcement? It can't be a coincidence."

Declan shared another look with Remi. After his call

with Cussler they'd spent the next few hours talking out his theory and going over what they knew.

Once again, Madi didn't let the exchange lie.

"There's more," she stated.

Declan nodded.

"For the last few years the Fixers organization has been popping up in our lives. From talk about men in suits to men in suits actually showing up as hired guns, they've been around. I have no doubt that the man at Waypoint Bar was a Fixer, the two men and woman on Main Street were Fixers, and even Lydia and the men at Heartland were Fixers. But, what is the *only* thing we know about them?"

"They do what they're paid to do," Desmond offered.

"Which means that *someone* out there is pulling the strings."

"But why?" Madi asked. "And to what end?"

Declan sat up straighter and then domed his hands over his lap.

Remi knew what he was about to say and yet goose bumps erupted across her skin when he said it.

"The woman outside of Claire's Café wasn't just attacked. She was pistol-whipped in the face. The man inside the café, Sam, was shot in the arm. The *side* of the arm. And Joe Langley had his leg broken. Badly." Silence filled the room so quickly Remi felt suffocated by it. Declan caused that silence with his deafening theory.

She looked at Madi and the scar that had been created by being pistol-whipped.

She looked at Caleb, remembering the scar across his arm from a bullet grazing it.

She looked at Desmond, the man who had grown up with a limp after having his leg broken from the sheer force of a man twice his size.

No one moved.

Declan had to bring the conversation home.

"I think everything that has happened in the last week is because someone is sending us, the Nash family, a very personal message."

MADI TOUCHED HER scar. Caleb rolled his shoulder back. Desmond put his hand on his knee. Then the three did something that only they seemed to be able to do on occasion.

They said the same thing at the same time.

"Why?"

Remi's brown eyes found his. Sometimes he believed they were a dark amber, beautiful and dangerous depending. Her brow was pinched, expression thoughtful. This was a question they'd already tried to tackle in the early hours of the morning. In fact, the case had become the only thing they'd talked about since Cussler had called.

Yet, here they were with no clear answers.

"One theory is someone is trying to rattle us. Maybe someone from an old case is ticked off at Caleb or me. Maybe someone is angry with Des because of the work he's been doing with the foundation. Maybe it's a blast from the past who's angry with Madi."

"But we know who it is," Caleb said. "It's the Fixers. We find them, we find answers."

Even though he said it, they both knew that was a tall

order. As much as it pained Declan to admit, finding the Fixers was a damn near impossible feat. Over the years they'd managed to catch a few, but once behind bars, the Fixers died by their own hands or another Fixer.

That was how their reputation had grown so much and so quickly.

They rarely got caught and, even if they did, they took their job, client and any other nefarious details with them to the grave.

Des had had a run-in with who they believed to be the leader of the Fixers in the last dealings with the group before now. He adopted a look of deep concentration and equal skepticism.

"The only time I was offered an answer from them, the cost would have been Riley and her sister's lives." He shook his head. "And that option was given to me by the man with the scar on his hand."

Declan sighed. The man they thought was the Fixer's head honcho had a scar in the shape of an X on his hand. It was identical to the scar the triplets' captor had had on his own hand when he'd taken them. This discovery was one of the main reasons Declan had been unable to completely walk away from trying to solve the case again.

"Which gives weight to the theory that someone has been playing with us for a while now." He ran a hand through his hair and then curved it down to run the top of his knuckles against the stubble beneath his chin. Frustration coursed through him. How he wished to be back in bed with Remi at his side.

"It could be him." Madi's voice was soft as she said

it, and Declan heard the pain. "It could be the man who took us."

That had been another theory. The triplets' abductor was toying with them. Declan didn't put too much stock in that possibility, and Caleb voiced the reason for that.

"Getting away with taking and scarring three little kids, who also happen to have a father in law enforcement, once, was a miracle on its own. For him to come back to mess with us would be an idiotic thing to do. He might as well throw self-preservation out the window."

Declan agreed. What would be the reasoning behind doing that? Especially all these years later?

"But no one knows why you were taken in the first place."

Everyone turned to Remi. Her cheeks tinted at the sudden attention, but she remained focused.

"When you were kids. No one ever figured out *why* you were taken." She straightened in her seat. "Because you're right. It was a miracle the guy never got caught. Everyone in town was looking for you, including your dad, the county's best detective at the time. *Everyone* was looking for you." She turned to Declan. "Which meant no one was looking for Justin Redman's attacker, someone who also was never found. How sure are you that Justin's death was an accident?"

Declan opened his mouth to answer. Nothing came out. Caleb also seemed to be at a loss. In the shadow of the abduction they'd never focused on the case that their father had abandoned.

"You think we were taken as a distraction," Madi spelled out. "So Dad wouldn't look into Justin's attack?"

Remi shrugged.

"If Cooper Mann didn't try to take Lydia, then he probably didn't put that note in the wall at the cabin, either. He was telling the truth and probably heard about it from a Fixer at the bar, knowing it would eventually get back to one of you. Whether they are toying with you all or not, Justin Redman has to have *some* kind of significance to all of this. Right? Why else go through the trouble of painting a note in a wall?"

Declan's heart rate sped up. The wheels in his head began to turn. For a moment no one spoke.

Had Remi just found one of their missing pieces?

Chapter Eighteen

"This is a bad plan."

"You've already said that. Three times now."

"Because it *is* a bad plan."

"For the record, I never said it was a good plan."

Declan snorted.

"Well, that doesn't help me feel better."

Remi ran her fingers through her hair and then tried to flatten the parts of it she'd pinned back. They'd had an eventful day. Some of it had included going back to Heartland. Remi had stayed stone silent as she'd led him to her childhood room. She'd kept that silence while finding the clothes she needed and changed. Declan had gone behind her, packing her bag with things he thought she might need for the foreseeable future. When she eyed him with a question seconds from her lips, he'd told her the simple truth.

"Sorry, Huds, you're stuck with me until this whole thing gets sorted out."

Remi hadn't fought him then, but he was back to fighting her hours later.

They were sitting in the parking lot of Waypoint

Bar in Kilwin. He was in his best pair of dark jeans, a
black button-up at her request and had on his vacation-
only dark blue Stetson. His sheriff's badge was in his
back pocket. The blazer in the back seat would hide his
shoulder holster.

Remi wasn't armed, which didn't mean she couldn't
do some damage. She was decked out in a sheer white
blouse that dipped low and tucked into a pair of navy
pants—which he noted matched his hat—with legs so
wide Declan had thought it was a long skirt at first.
She'd chosen black flats that wrapped around her ankles
and lipstick that reminded him of a bull's-eye. One he
very much wanted to hit.

"I wore this to a party one of my clients threw for
Towne & Associates after I cleaned up the absolute
mess that was their finances," she'd said after debuting
the look. "I packed it on the off chance I could convince
Molly to go out while I was in town."

Now, looking at her in the glow from Waypoint's
lone light at the back of the parking lot, Declan found
the outfit to be too much. Just like the plan.

Remi sighed and slapped him lightly on the shoulder.

"Stop it. Stop that broodiness right now. We need to
do this and do it right." She motioned to her outfit and
his. Her brows drew in together. She rolled her shoulders back. Then she reminded him why he'd agreed to
the bad plan in the first place. "Justin Redman said he
was supposed to meet Dean Lawson the day he was attacked. No one ever got around to asking Mr. Lawson
what for. Now we can, thanks to your brothers pulling
some hefty favors to find this Lawson guy and get us

a meeting *twenty-five years* after the fact." She motioned to their outfits again. At the movement his attention redirected to the curve of her breast. Remi was nice enough not to call him out for it. "If Lawson can't give us any information we can use about Justin Redman, then we can leave him be and mingle with the rest of the crowd and see if we can't at least find something about the man who told Cooper about the note in the wall. If you go in with a sheriff's badge on your chest, guns blazing, I don't think we'll get the response we want. Right now we just look like two people on a date. It's not like everyone in the city knows you're the Wildman county sheriff."

Declan saw the logic in it, but he didn't have to like it.

Remi let out a frustrated huff.

"You told Julian to keep watch on Madi. You have Desmond with your mom. Caleb is with his wife and son. Jazz is working with your chief deputy to find Lydia and the people who have been attacking strangers and my family home." She reached out and took his chin in her hand. It was soft and warm. "You told me earlier that you're not leaving me. I'm telling you right now that *I'm* not leaving *you*."

She kept his gaze for a moment before letting go.

Then she was smiling.

"So, now that that's out of the way, can we please go in already? I have to pee. Again."

Despite every reservation he had, which numbered many, Declan chuckled.

"Yes, ma'am."

Declan had already been told that Waypoint had lost

its law enforcement hangout roots, but it was still odd to see in person. What had once been walls covered in framed pictures of fallen heroes, graduating classes, candid stills from on the job and an assortment of police memorabilia had now been swapped for a moodier aesthetic. Posters from old movies, handmade wall art and pictures of people relaxing after, he assumed, a long day on the job surrounded a clientele who were in varying stages of after-work comfort. Declan led Remi past two dartboards mounted against the interior faded brick, a dimly lit pool table, a wall lined with flat screens, clusters of tables, and up to the massive bar that lined the back wall. No one paid them any mind as they walked through. Not even a wayward glace as Remi stopped just shy of the counter and turned to him.

"That's him," she whispered, trying and failing to be covert about her head nod. The man in question was sitting hunched over in the middle of the bar, a few feet from them. Declan would have questioned her ability to pick him out so easily from the angle if it hadn't been for his hair. Stark white and falling past his shoulders. Just as it had been in the picture from his online profile and the several magazine pieces written about him.

Dean Lawson was a businessman, like Desmond. However, unlike Declan's brother, Lawson was in real estate and was more known for throwing extravagant parties for wealthy clients and driving sports cars with bikini models than charitable giving. His idea of helping the community, as far as Declan could tell from a general Google search, was putting attractive people in expensive houses. The latest article about him had been his announcement that he was passing his business on to his son. They'd been lucky he was visiting Kilwin before heading back to his current home of Miami.

Declan was hoping they'd be even luckier before the night ended.

"How do we play this?" Remi asked. "Good cop, bad cop?"

Declan raised his eyebrow at that.

"We're just going to see if he knows anything about Justin that can help us. We don't really need a good cop or a bad cop."

Remi snorted.

"That's what they always say."

"They?" he asked with a laugh. She nodded. Her eyes darted back to Lawson. She was excited. Declan couldn't much blame her. Just the *chance* of a lead could get his adrenaline going.

"Okay, there, hotshot, why don't we sit next to him and just talk first?"

"All right, but if you want me to turn up the heat or to help you, just say 'coconut.' That can be our safe word."

"Coconut? How am I supposed to work that into a conversation?"

Remi shrugged.

"If anything goes wrong, then you'll find a way."

She threw him a teasing grin and nodded toward Lawson.

The seats on either side of him were unoccupied. Declan touched the small of Remi's back before passing her and sliding onto the bar stool to the man's left while she took the right.

Declan noticed two things about Mr. Lawson from the get-go. One, he was working on at least his third drink. Two empty shot glasses hadn't been cleared yet from in front of him. The current glass his hand was wrapped around looked to contain whiskey. Two, the man matched the mood of three drinks. His shoulders were drooped over, his elbow propped up on the counter-top, and his gaze was on the liquid of his drink. The word *dejected* popped into Declan's head at the sight of him.

When he dragged his eyes up to meet Declan's, his expression was blank.

"Mr. Lawson," he greeted, offering his hand to shake. "I'm Declan Nash and this is Remi. Thank you for meeting us."

Dean Lawson's handshake was a half-hearted affair. One he didn't extend to Remi, who gave Declan a disapproving look over the man's shoulder.

"You know, I hadn't been back to Kilwin in ten years and then I'm in town for less than a week and everyone wants a piece." He took a sip of his drink. "What a wild ride."

Again Remi gave Declan a look.

"Well, thank you for coming out to meet us, then," he said, using his cordial voice reserved for press conferences. "We won't keep you long."

Lawson waved his hand dismissively.

"Don't worry, son, tonight is the last time I worry

about managing my time. But whatever you're going to ask, better go ahead and ask it."

Declan didn't like Dean Lawson, he decided. Then again, he didn't need to like him to ask a question.

"Do you remember a man named Justin Redman?" he started, easing into it.

Lawson nodded.

"I do."

He didn't make any attempt to elaborate. Declan kept on.

"Twenty-five years ago he was attacked at a gas station by an unidentified man. Justin was killed in a car accident before the case could be investigated. The only information we had about the incident was the day it happened Justin said in a statement he was on the way to meet you. Do you remember why?"

Lawson ran his index finger up and down the side of his glass. He didn't look to Declan as he answered.

"Funnily enough, I don't remember why exactly he wanted to meet then. I remember the man, though." His face became pinched. "A child in men's clothes. That's what he reminded me of. A man who, for whatever reason, thought he was more than he was. An annoying little twerp." He laughed. It was unkind.

Remi's look of concern rivaled Declan's own confusion. Dean Lawson was showing signs of disgust and hostility for a man who had died over two decades ago.

Lawson took the last long drink of his whiskey and shook the glass at the passing bartender. He was an older man who paid no attention to Declan or Remi. Not that either had planned on drinking, but the oversight added to the list of reasons Declan liked the old Waypoint Bar over the new version of it.

The bartender refilled his glass.

Lawson smiled down at the new drink.

"Did you know that I grew up in Kilwin?" he asked. "Not too far from this bar, actually. My dad was in sales and my mom inherited all of her father's money in lieu of an actual job. I grew up watching my dad, a proud and honest man, continue to work himself to the bone to provide for a family already provided for while my mother couldn't understand why he resented her. *Then* he died and Mom finally understood that all he'd been trying to do was show her the best things in life are earned, not bought." Lawson gave Declan a look of such loathing he nearly felt it as a physical thing. "So, in a drastic one-eighty to honor my father she decided I wouldn't see an ounce of her or his money ever. Not a dime, not a penny." Declan didn't miss his grip tighten around his glass. "Now, that might seem like an okay and even normal thing for most families but, you have to understand, I'd already spent my life relying on that money. My father was always away on business trips and my mother had already made the choice to make my life as easy as possible. When she decided that was a mistake and one she wouldn't continue to make? I was *days* away from striking out on my own."

He took a drink.

Declan's body was tensing on reflex, readying for something. He just wasn't sure what yet. Remi's body language had changed, too. She sat taller, more rigid. Neither had any idea what was going on.

Lawson finished his most recent drink and shook his head.

"Boy, was I stubborn about still sticking to the plan I'd made when I'd had the money and, boy, was I bad at it. It wasn't long at all before I was going to bed hungry in a crappy little apartment, filled with worry over what I'd do next. Then one night everything changed. One night I decided something that has been the guiding motivation of everything I've ever done since." Lawson shook his glass with one decisive shake. "There is no honor in starving, so why be honorable if that's what you'll get?"

Declan couldn't stay quiet any longer.

"Why are you telling us this?"

Lawson went back to staring at his drink. When he spoke next he sounded almost wistful.

"Because I wanted someone to know that, while I don't regret the things I've done over the last few decades to build the life I've lived, I did want someone to understand why I did them."

"And what are the things you've done?" Remi asked.

He didn't look up from his drink as he answered her.

"I made money and I protected that money. No matter the cost."

"Justin Redman didn't die in an accident, did he?" Declan formed it as a question, but his gut was already telling him it was true. "You killed him."

Lawson didn't deny it.

"The man was an idiot. He gets into a fight with one of my suppliers and then has the nerve to give a statement saying he was supposed to be meeting up with me after?" Lawson's anger was as potent as his loathing had been earlier. Declan readied for anything, including body slamming the man against the ground behind them if he even so much as blinked at Remi now or dropped his hands off the countertop. "Our standing arrangement was supposed to be confidential and only one of the many other confidential things he knew. Once your father was tasked with finding his attacker, I knew it was only a matter of time before Justin slipped up and damned me and everything I'd been working for. Deciding to kill him was easy. It was the other parts that were hard."

He laughed. It held no humor and sounded weaker than the one before.

"I thought I'd made it out. I really did. I went twenty-five years without ever hearing Justin's name and, yet, one week back in town and he's one of several names I've heard that I never wanted to again. I shouldn't have come back home." He sighed, pushed his drink away from him and grimaced. Then he was looking squarely at Declan. "You know, I saw you and your siblings, out on Main Street when I was in town once. The triplets were tiny, loud little things. Inseparable and a spectacle all in one. Everyone paid attention to them because of how rare triplets are, especially in Overlook. I admit, I was one of them. To this day I've not met another triplet set. But you? The eldest brother and singleton? No one paid you any mind. You weren't special. Not like they were."

Declan's hands had balled into fists. He couldn't look away from the man who would have been his father's age, staring at him without an ounce of fear of the consequences to what he was saying.

Dean Lawson didn't waver one bit.

Even when what he said next changed absolutely everything.

"That's why I paid him to kidnap you, instead. But he didn't listen to me, did he?"

Chapter Nineteen

Surprised wasn't the right word.

Angry wasn't, either.

Remi watched as Declan's face hardened into an emotion that made her feelings fall somewhere between the two. Fear didn't even register. Why would it?

Dean Lawson was just a sad man in a bar with a drink never that far from his fingertips.

A sad man who'd just said he had paid to have Declan kidnapped which, as history showed, hadn't worked out.

"Come again?" Declan's voice was ice.

Lawson sighed. The hunch he'd already been sitting with became more pronounced.

"Michael Nash was one of those hard-nosed detectives you see on old cop shows. The ones who never lose. If he'd gotten ahold of Justin, he would have gotten ahold of me. There was only one thing in the world that could have distracted him. Taking his kid." He pointed at Declan and shook his head. "But…" He glanced at the bartender. The older man was staring as he wiped a glass dry. Remi wondered if he had heard the patron's admission. "Things escalated. And now we're here."

Declan moved his blazer. She knew beneath it was his gun. They'd come here to get more insight into Justin Redman, and here they were sitting with the man who had paid to make the abduction possible.

"Who did you pay?" Declan's voice was unrecognizable.

Lawson shared a look with Remi. Or at least she thought it was with her. Instead, his eyes skirted to the person on the bar stool to the right of her. He had been in a conversation with a woman on the other side of him when they'd first sat down. Now the couple had gone silent and still. The bartender had also changed states. He placed a still-wet glass on the bar top and kept his dishrag in hand.

The hair on the back of Remi's neck started to stand.

Declan was understandably focused on Lawson, just as she had been, but now other details were blaring. The music that had been somewhat loud when they walked in had now softened. The movement of the bar's patrons eating, drinking and talking had lessened. The bar was quiet enough for her to hear the TV at the other side of the room.

Now that her focus wasn't homed in on Lawson's every word, Remi could tell something was off. *Very* off.

And Lawson was a part of it.

He wasn't answering Declan's question, even though he'd just incriminated himself by supplying information he hadn't really needed to give.

Surely he knew that Declan and the sheriff's department would go at him full force now?

Why did he suddenly seem so hesitant?

"I asked a question," Declan thrummed.

Again, Lawson kept quiet.

Something hit the floor between Lawson and Remi. She glanced down, body already taut with nerves.

Nerves that escalated so quickly it was a struggle not to openly gasp.

Blood.

That was what had hit the ground.

And it was coming from beneath Lawson's blazer.

"Coconut." The word came out before Remi could stop it. Then she chanted it. "Coconut. Coconut. Coconut."

Declan tore his eyes away from Lawson. Remi shook her head. The man between them chuckled. He finally took a long look at her.

That was when Remi *really* saw it. The pale skin, the pain.

The acceptance.

Now she knew why he'd freely admitted to what he'd done.

He was already dead.

"You can't escape them," he said. "He blamed me for complicating his life. He blames the Nashes for ruining it."

"We need to leave," Remi whispered across him, urgency making her heartbeat take off in a gallop.

"For over two decades he planned a way to find his justice." Lawson shook his head. "You'll only leave this place if it's a part of that plan. And, boy, is he big on plans."

Declan was off his bar stool in a flash. The movement seemed to be tied to every person inside the bar. Chairs scraped against wood and glasses clinked against tables as the entirety of Waypoint stood. They all had their guns out before Declan could pull his.

And they all were aimed at Remi.

Lawson was the only one who remained seated.

He turned back to his drink.

Remi, wide-eyed, looked at Declan.

He was furious.

"This was a trap. One we set up ourselves," he said through gritted teeth. "I should have never brought you."

Remi had opened her mouth to say she was sorry for pushing them to come since it had obviously been a bad plan after all when she was interrupted by a man breaking away from a group in the middle of the room. He was dressed in an expensive suit and smiling.

"We didn't give you much choice, now did we?" the man said. "After we realized the value of Miss Hudson, we knew that an attack against her would only make you stick that much closer to her side. Even taking her to a bar for a seemingly insignificant meeting." He stopped a few feet from them. Then he held out his hands and lowered them. Every patron around them put away their guns and sat back down.

Then it was just the three of them standing.

"If you hadn't brought her, then we would have. And killed every innocent person we had to to do it," he continued. "*This* was the best option you could have hoped for."

"I've been looking for you for a while now," Declan said. "The man with the scar on his hand who seems to pop up when us Nashes are involved."

Remi looked down at the man's hand. Sure enough she could see the scar in the shape of an X on it.

He was the leader of the Fixers.

And they were apparently in their den.

The man kept smiling.

"Maybe it's you all who keep popping up in my business. Did you ever think of that?"

Declan's hands were fisted. Remi wanted to hold them, but didn't want to move and start a fight.

"You're too young to have carried out the abduction," he said. "What's your part in all of this now? What do you want with us?"

The man's smile twisted into a nasty smirk.

"*I'm* here to give you some choices. Some hard choices. Then we'll be leaving and you'll never see me again."

Declan wasn't pleased with that answer.

"Let her go and I'll make all the choices you want."

The man shook his head. Then he looked at Remi.

"She's the one who has to make the first choice."

Declan started to move toward her to, she guessed, shield her from the man, his words and the consequences they'd bring. The man in the suit didn't have to lift a hand to stop him. Half of the bar raised their guns again. Declan held up his hands and stopped.

He actually growled.

"It's okay," she said. Then to the man in the suit, she said, "You clearly like the sound of your own voice so why don't you go ahead and give me your bad-guy spiel so you can hear it some more." The man's eyebrow rose. "Sorry, do you want me to sound more like a damsel? Do you want me to cry?"

"Huds," Declan warned.

I'm sassing because of pregnancy hormones and straight up fear, she wanted to explain. Instead, she tried to simmer down.

The man actually sniggered at her.

"I guess it shouldn't surprise me that you have some bite. You *did* manage to escape my men yesterday."

"After I shot one," she added, failing at keeping her sass in check.

The man nodded, conceding.

"You did, and it was such a bold decision given the odds. Which makes this next part interesting for me." He cleared his throat and clasped his hands behind his back. "This entire organization was made with the sole purpose of destroying the Nash family. From root to stem, every job taken, every connection made, has been a means to an end…for some of us. Myself? I'd like to think we're worth more than a revenge plot. But, for now, here I am to get us all to the next stage." His smile dropped and suddenly he was the image of a consummate professional. "You, Remi Hudson, can do one of two things. You can either come with me willingly to be bait for Declan and the triplets to come save you later, or you can refuse and I'll kill Declan and you'll still be bait for the triplets later. The choice is yours."

Remi went ramrod straight. Declan cussed and started telling her no.

She didn't listen.

"So I can either die now or die later? Not much of a choice."

The man shrugged.

"Think of it like this, if you leave voluntarily *he* won't die now and might even save *you* later. It's probably your best option."

"She's not going anywhere with you," Declan yelled. The man paid him no mind again.

"If I go with you, what's to stop your happy helpers from killing him the moment we leave?"

"Nothing, but we'd like his help for this next part. He's the best candidate to convince his siblings to meet us all at Well Water Cabin. Alone."

A shiver went down Remi's spine.

"Why do you want to go there?" Declan had to ask.

"Because it's poetic, I suppose. Because we can. Now, Miss Hudson, make your choice."

Remi looked at Declan.

Beautiful, soulful green eyes. Smart and cunning and, most of all, kind.

Declan Nash was a good man. He would be an even greater father. But to be that, to have that chance, Remi had to keep herself alive. Just as she had to keep him alive, too. Since she wasn't in law enforcement, didn't have a weapon and was standing in a room filled with at least fifteen people who weren't afraid to use theirs, making her choice was laughably simple.

"I'll go."

EVERY MAN AND woman had their weapons back up.

Some were itching to use them.

Declan knew the feeling, but reality was biting him in the backside. He made a rough estimate that there was no way he could get Remi out before one of the fifteen or so guns went off and bullets rained down on them both. Even if he became a human shield, the odds weren't in their favor that he could get her out without being hurt. He also figured there was no way he could get her safely out the back door behind the bar which, he assumed, led to a kitchen or office and eventually to an exit.

In fact, any way he sliced it, there was no good option to save Remi.

Rage boiled beneath his skin. Helplessness only made it hotter.

He should have never sought out information on Justin Redman. Going to Well Water to look for the note in the first place had been a mistake. Just as going back with Remi to find it had been.

He should have locked Remi and him up in his room. Stayed together beneath the sheets.

Definitely not brought her along to Waypoint Bar.

"There's no way in hell you're going," he told her, chancing a slight movement that angled him between her and the man in the suit. She smiled. It made every part of him wish he could protect every part of her.

"I am. And you're going to let me." She lowered her voice to an almost-whisper. "Who knows Well Water better than you do?"

It was a question that hung in the air as the distance between them grew. Declan watched helplessly as his future family walked away from him.

Remi stopped at the man's shoulder. When she spoke, there was fire in her words and she let the entire room hear them.

"I may not have a badge or a gun but if I find out anyone so much as touched him after we left, you will never see me coming. I'll rip you and your cute little suit to shreds."

The man in the suit chuckled and nodded. He motioned to a woman at the table nearest him. She made her way over and then led Remi out.

Remi didn't look back at him.

Which was good.

Declan was doing all he could to keep from running after her and taking out as many guns as he could along the way. And maybe the Fixers around them knew that. Some pulled their guns higher.

When Remi and the woman were out of the bar the man in the suit moved closer. The smile he'd given Remi's sass was gone. His tone reminded Declan of a tired teacher.

"You will bring Madi, Caleb and Desmond to Well Water Cabin at midnight. You will tell no one else where you are going or why. You will lie if anyone asks where Remi is and you will do it convincingly."

"And if it's just me who shows up?"

The man in the suit shook his head.

"That's not part of the plan."

"And that's not a good answer."

He shrugged.

"I'm not here to give you what you want, Declan.

I'm here to tell you the only chance you have at saving one family is to sacrifice the other. Like Remi, you have a choice here. Show up at Well Water with your siblings or don't."

"You're just going to kill us all when we get there," Declan said, trying to tamp down his anger. He motioned to Lawson behind them. He'd seen the blood after Remi had started yelling "coconut." Then he'd pieced it all together. They'd done something to Lawson, hurt him. Now he was dying. "Did you give him the same ultimatum? Show up and die, or don't show up and have someone you love die?"

"No," the man answered, voice clipped. "He never had a choice."

Declan flexed his hands, uncurling and curling them into fists.

"If you're really going to let me go, then let me take him with me."

Dean Lawson was a walking and talking answer. He'd paid for the abduction, which meant he knew the man with the scar who'd done it. Because Declan didn't for one second think that the man across from him now would tell him. And, honestly, if he did Declan would have a hard time believing him.

Lawson was the only silver lining of everything that was happening. A small, barely there sliver.

The man in the suit's lips curled up into a grin.

"Like I said, Dean never had a choice," he said. "He was always meant to die here surrounded by us, an empire made from nothing."

Lawson must have known that.

That was why he'd told Declan and Remi what he'd done.

And that was why he hadn't told them who he'd paid. He couldn't. Not with a room filled with Fixers.

He might have been dying, but he hadn't wanted to die yet.

Neither did Declan.

"I'll go," he said, repeating Remi's words.

The man in the suit nodded. He didn't flinch as Declan moved toward him and instead walked him out of the bar. Remi's car was still parked in the same spot they'd left it in, but she and the woman who had gone after her were nowhere to be seen. In fact, there was no one around at all.

It was just him and the man in the suit.

Declan could take him right then and there. Could pull his gun out, could tackle him, could dish out a punch that splayed him out on the concrete, but Declan found that he believed in the man's sincerity about what would happen if he didn't show up at Well Water Cabin.

He'd lose Remi.

He'd lose his baby.

Nothing was worth that.

Instead, Declan decided to throw himself into the next part of the plan he was being forced into. He started to walk away, but the man in the suit had some last words for him.

"You've seen us over the years. You've seen what we do and you know how good we are at doing it. There's also a lot you haven't seen. There's a lot you don't know.

Don't underestimate us, Sheriff." It wasn't bragging. It was a warning. One he recapped. "If you or your siblings tell anyone about what's going on, we'll know, and it won't end well. For any of you or your families."

Declan almost decked the man then.

"I've met a lot of criminals in my life," he said with barely contained rage. "Do you know that most of them have a code? Have *some* honor?"

The man in the suit sighed. He actually sighed. Then he met Declan's eyes with a pensive stare.

"You've seen us over the years, and I've seen you Nashes over the years, too. I've seen you drown. I've seen you shot. I've seen you run into the darkness, run into flames, and run into places where the odds were never in your favor. You may think of yourselves as a normal family dealing in bad luck, but me? I see you as survivors, even if it's by the skin of your teeth. I wouldn't bet against you Nashes. You shouldn't, either."

Declan felt his eyebrow rise. The man in the suit gave a brief smile.

"I may not have *honor*, Mr. Nash," he continued. "But I am smart. Putting all four of you in one place while threatening your partners and children? Well, anyone would be a fool to believe with certainty that you'd lose in the end. I'm just trying to remain realistic."

Pride stirred in Declan's chest at that, but he made sure not to show it as he asked one last question.

One that he already knew the answer to.

"Your client, the one who hired you to orchestrate

all of this—he's the one who took the triplets, isn't he? He's come back for them."

The man in the suit was solemn as he answered.

"He's come back for all of you."

Chapter Twenty

Declan went to Caleb's house first.

It was on the Nash Family Ranch and had been rebuilt with the help of the siblings. There was a wraparound porch with a swing on it that Declan himself had hung. That was where he found his brother sitting with his wife, Nina, and their son, Parker.

It was just after supper and they looked content.

When they saw Declan they all smiled, even Parker.

It tore at his heart as he lied.

"Hey, Caleb, I need your help on something," he said after they greeted each other. "Do you mind coming with me?"

Nina was readjusting Parker who had started to squirm, so she didn't see her husband's look of concern. Declan didn't have that triplet telepathy but he knew Caleb could feel something was majorly off. He ran his hand over his wife's back and dipped in for a kiss against her temple.

"Sure thing," he said to Declan. Then to her, Caleb said, "Nina, why don't you two go over to Mom's while we're gone. It would be the perfect time to put together that plastic play set she's been needing help with for the kids."

"Oh, you mean the one you boys were supposed to put together but always seem to have something better to do?" she responded, teasing clear in her voice. She sighed, all dramatic. "I suppose I always knew us ladies were the more capable ones. Plus, Parker took too long of a nap today and I don't see him going to bed anytime soon. Maybe this will tire him out."

Caleb and Declan helped her get Parker and his things into the car. While he gave Nina a quick kiss, Declan ruffed up Parker's hair and then gave him a tight hug. Caleb, seeing this, spent more time with the goodbye.

It wasn't until they were in the car and heading to pick up Desmond that Caleb turned to him.

"When you went to that bar you told us all to watch our families because they weren't safe. What's going on? And where's Remi? Why are we in her car but she's not here?"

"I can't tell you yet," Declan said with the stiffness of holding on to a world of worries for far too long. "We need to get Desmond and Madi first."

Caleb didn't argue. He didn't question. He listened to his big brother and Declan loved him for it.

Desmond's house had been built behind the main home they'd grown up in and their mother currently lived in but, from Declan's earlier instructions, he and his wife were at the main house. Nina got to the house a few seconds before they did and Caleb jumped out of the car to help her and Parker into the house. Desmond came back outside with him as Declan hung back.

He loved his mother dearly, but if Caleb was picking up on his tension, then their mother would, too.

Desmond's limp only made Declan feel worse. It must have shown. Both brothers shared a look between them after seeing Declan.

All three got into the car in silence.

Then they were on Winding Road and heading toward Hidden Hills Inn.

"Julian will know something's wrong," Desmond said without prompting. "He won't let her leave without an explanation. Not unless he knows she won't be in any danger."

Declan gritted his teeth.

"Then she'll have to lie."

"It's that bad?" Caleb asked.

"It'll be worse if anyone thinks something's wrong."

That was enough to keep the boys quiet until they made it to the bed-and-breakfast Madi and Julian lived at and ran. There were no guests currently at the inn, but as soon as they cut the engine Julian appeared in the doorway of the house.

"Let me go get her," Caleb said, grabbing Declan's shoulder to keep him from getting up. "I'm closer with Julian than you two."

Declan didn't argue that. Julian had saved Caleb's life and, since then, the two had become close. In fact, Parker's middle name was Julian. Something that had made the older Julian tear up when he'd found out.

Their friendship was put to the test that night. Dec-

Ian and Desmond couldn't hear what they said, but it was clear that Julian knew something was wrong, too, and wasn't about to let Madi be a part of it. Then Madi appeared. She joined the conversation and must have strengthened whatever argument Caleb had been making.

Then all three went inside.

Only Madi and Caleb came back out a minute later.

Caleb slid into the back seat and Madi buckled into the front.

They left Hidden Hills Inn and were quiet until they got to where Declan hadn't been in years.

He parked next to the river he had drowned in once. It was on land that no one currently lived on. He got out and the triplets followed.

The night was peaceful and cold.

Declan looked at his watch and began.

"I'm about to give you a lot of information really fast. Information that will be a lot to understand, but we're running low on time so I need you all to take it with a nod and let me keep going. Okay?"

They nodded in unison. No one was smiling. They wouldn't be after he was done, either.

"Justin Redman was supposed to meet Dean Lawson. That meeting was supposed to be secret. Lawson has been, as far as I can guess, dealing with drugs to make his fortune. Or, at least, he was back then. Justin got into a fight with one of his suppliers and then said Lawson's name in an official report. Lawson said he knew if Dad looked into the attack at all that Justin would eventually lead him to what Lawson had been doing and everything he worked for would be taken away. So, he decided to pay someone to abduct me to distract Dad. Lawson said that the man he paid didn't listen and, well, we know what happened instead."

Guilt surged through Declan. Guilt so strong he nearly stopped talking. He should have been the one taken. Not them.

"It's not your fault," Madi said, picking up on his thoughts. "Keep going."

Declan sighed.

"Lawson only told me this because he was dying and he was only still alive to get me and Remi to the bar. It was filled with Fixers." At this part he hesitated. Three pairs of true-blue eyes searched his face.

They were adults now. They had children and spouses. Careers, mortgages, and dental insurance.

Declan had walked Madi down the aisle at her wedding in the backyard of the inn she'd made into a home and business.

He'd been at Caleb's graduation and then sworn him in when he'd become a detective.

He'd stood, arm around Desmond, and looked up at a building that had been erected for the foundation he'd created that helped thousands of people daily.

Declan knew they were adults.

Knew that they could handle themselves. Knew they'd grown into thriving individuals.

Yet, standing there looking at them so close to where their father used to take them all fishing as a family, Declan saw only the little kids who had snuck out to a park to play a game of hide-and-seek and had reappeared three days later all grown-up.

How he wished with all his heart and soul he could have changed their fates.

He took another breath and then ripped off the bandage.

"The man who abducted you is back and he wants us to go to Well Water Cabin tonight to die."

There was a moment where no one said a word.

Then that was the last silence for a while.

"Who is he?" Caleb asked.

"I don't know. Lawson wouldn't say."

"He hired the Fixers, though?" Desmond asked.

Declan nodded.

"Apparently they've been in his back pocket for years. All the bad stuff that's gone down with us all? Them, at his order. I don't know why he's coming after us all now, but he is. The man in the suit, the leader we keep running into, said they'll kill everyone we love if we tell a soul about the meeting."

Madi took a small step forward. She put her hand over her heart.

"You want us to go," she said, voice soft, "because they have Remi, don't they?"

He nodded.

"They know something I should have told you yesterday." He gave them a small smile. Happy for the news, angry at how he had to give it. "She's pregnant… with my kid."

Madi was the first to move. She threw her arms around Declan. Caleb and Desmond weren't far behind.

"Oh, Declan, I'm so happy for you," Madi said into his chest.

"Same here, big guy," Desmond said.

"You'll make an awesome dad," Caleb finished.

"Thanks, guys."

The warmth of familial love spread through him at the words. At the group hug. At the way the future seemed brighter with the thought of a baby in it.

Then that warmth cooled until it was ice.

The Nash children stepped back and all joy was gone.

"I'm not like the Fixers. I'm not going to force you to come to Well Water with me. My best guess is this man wants to talk and then he'll kill us all. But there's no guarantee he won't kill us all the moment we drive up." Declan felt the resolution in his heart before the words to back it up left his lips. "But I'm going. Even if it's only to give Remi a better chance at escaping. I just—I wanted you all to know. You've deserved answers for most of your lives. I wanted you to at least get some of them."

The triplets didn't even look at each other.

Madi spoke first.

"You're wrong," she said with bite. "Saving your family, getting our answers, and finally giving that son of a bitch what's coming to him. We deserve it all."

"She's right," Desmond said with vigor. "We're going and we're going to save Remi and we're going to finally put this mystery to rest."

Caleb nodded. Declan was surprised to see him smirk. In fact, he surprised to see all of them so calm. The man who had scarred them, locked them up and changed all of their lives because of this was waiting for them.

Waiting to kill them.

Yet, there they were.

Suddenly those three children looked exactly as they should have to him.

Two men and a woman ready for justice.

Caleb captured the sentiment well.

"Whoever this man is, whatever his reason is for wanting us, he's overlooked one devastating fact. We're grown-up now and we won't be as easy to push around."

Madi and Desmond agreed.

Declan smiled at this brothers and sister.

"Then it's settled," he said. "Now, we have less than three hours to come up with a plan to find justice for our father, bring peace to our mother, get answers for us, and save the woman I love and our kid. Any objections?"

Not a one of them made a peep.

THE BASEMENT WASN'T as bad as Remi had pictured. In fact, in any other circumstance, she would have thought it was cozy.

A few steps from the stairs was a door that led into a spacious room with a kitchenette in the corner and an open door that showed a bathroom on the other side. The light fixtures were nice and did a good job of lighting up the place, and even the kitchenette was pleasing to look at.

What changed the feel of the room in such a sudden and violent way was the three small cots against the wall and the four locks on the door, reminding her just what the triplets had gone through all those years ago.

When the woman in the pantsuit locked all four locks, Remi quaked in fear. She was alone in the room and leaned into the privacy. She cried. She hoped she hadn't left Declan to die and she hoped she hadn't just led herself and their child to do the same.

She felt exhausted.

She felt helpless.

And then she felt sick.

Remi ran to the bathroom with tears blurring her vision and threw up in the sink.

Because of course morning sickness didn't take a break. Not even when she was being held captive. She tried to compose herself after the deed and instead was hit with another wave of nausea.

This time she threw up in the toilet.

After that she leaned against the wall and cried some more.

It wasn't until a man cleared his throat that Remi realized someone was in the doorway.

The man in the suit from Waypoint was holding a bottle of water and a packet of gum.

"There might be power now, but there's no running water in the house, I'm afraid," he said. "And if you die tonight I'd bet it would feel nicer to die with somewhat fresh-feeling breath."

He stepped back to let her out of the bathroom and shook the bottle when she didn't take it.

"Both are in sealed containers. Not taking them is only going to make *you* more uncomfortable. Not me."

Remi was thirsty and her mouth tasted awful. Denying either point didn't make them go away. She relented and took both, but not without a severe look she hoped hurt the man.

"Being kind to a pregnant woman you're about to kill doesn't make you a good person, you know," she said hotly.

The man shrugged.

"Who says I want to be a good person?"

That sent a shiver of fear down Remi's spine. Whether she wanted to feel it or not.

"But, if it makes you feel better, I won't be the one killing you. That's not part of the plan."

Remi opened the bottle, breaking its seal, and went back to the bathroom to wash her mouth out. When she came back she took a long drink of water and popped two pieces of gum.

Both made her feel light-years better.

So did her barb at the man.

"For someone who thinks they're so clever, it's interesting to find out you're nothing more than someone else's bitch."

The man snorted, trying to seem like he'd blown off the insult, but Remi saw it.

She saw the nostrils flare, saw the anger pass over him.

She'd hit a nerve.

Because she'd spoken the truth.

But the man was more disciplined than she had hoped. He was back to smiling.

"For being the bait that's going to lead almost an entire family to slaughter, you sure are cocky."

Remi wanted to say something clever, something

that hurt him, but she didn't have his discipline. She kept quiet and went to one of the cots, and he eventually left without another word.

Then there she sat for hours.

In that time she thought about her father, her brothers, her mother and stepfather, her job, and the Nashes. She thought about Declan and their unborn child the most.

By the time the door to the basement opened, Remi had come to a decision. The only catch was that they all had to survive the night.

Remi didn't recognize the man who walked in but she recognize did the scar on his hand.

The man who had taken the triplets.

The man who wanted them all to die.

And he'd come to see her first.

Chapter Twenty-One

There were at least twenty men and women wearing suits surrounding the cabin. It was such an odd sight to Declan. For the last decade Well Water had been forgotten by most of the world, a desolate structure that was visited by him only for the occasional maintenance. Before that it had been his father visiting. Before that it had been a circus.

Now the abandoned cabin in the woods had too many people in and around it. People dressed for the boardroom with guns in hand like they were going to war.

"If it all goes sideways I'm doing everything in my power to get Remi out," Declan said after he found a place to park among a cluster of inconspicuous cars and trucks. "That includes dying. And you're going to let me if that means you can get out, too."

No one rebuffed him, but Desmond tried to be reassuring.

"This will work. I know it will."

No one backed him up but no one disagreed.

They'd had three hours to come up with a plan to save Remi and themselves without weapons, without help, and without knowing how many people would be at the cabin.

Their plan was at best risky; at worst it was downright idiotic.

And it was all they had.

A man came to the door as Declan got out. He was sneering. It was the one man he'd chased across Main Street. He ran a hand through his red hair, exposing the holster and the gun in it against his side.

"Howdy, Sheriff. If you'd be so kind to allow my associates to check you all for any knives, guns, bombs, *et cetera*, that would be mighty kind of you." He was mocking them but Declan allowed the search. Just as his siblings did. The redhead seemed surprised that none of them had any weapons of any kind on them. No cell phones, either.

Those were back at the river, GPS on, and each holding video recordings for their families and law enforcement. They were hoping their plan would work but prepared if it didn't. Watching his siblings make their videos for their kids and spouses tore Declan apart. They'd noticed and told him again this was their choice to make and they'd made it.

Tonight, for better or worse, one nightmare would end.

Redhead led them inside and cut right to the living room. Declan felt the tension coming off the triplets. This was the first time Madi and Desmond had been back to Well Water since they'd escaped. For Caleb it had been a few years, but that didn't matter.

This place was their personal hell.

One that was filled to the brim with strangers waiting for them.

Among the crowd was the man in the suit. Still the fanciest in the group. He smiled when they stopped in front of him.

"You didn't bring any weapons and you didn't ask for any help. I don't know if you aren't that smart or if you all are just a bit too confident."

"You gave us terms and we followed them," Declan said. "I'd say that makes us, at least, respectful."

The man in the suit nodded. He was pleased.

"It does make everything go smoothly when you follow the rules."

Declan looked around the room. He knew where she probably was but still had to ask.

"Where's Remi?"

The man's smile faded. He became the ideal image of a businessman.

"She's downstairs with the man of the hour." He held up his hand to stop Declan from saying how much he didn't like that. "She's fine. We can go see her now."

He nodded to the people around them. Most stayed but Redhead, a woman with a sneer and three others followed. They walked behind their group as Declan followed the man in the suit to the only place that was ever an option for this horrible meeting.

Declan turned to his siblings as they got to the top of the stairs to the basement. He lowered his voice.

"You're not little kids anymore."

Caleb nodded. Desmond and Madi grabbed hands and stood straighter.

Then the Nash children followed the man in the suit down into the room they wanted to go in least. Right up to the smiling face of a man Declan had never seen.

Yet the triplets had.

Madi made a guttural, primal growl.

Caleb balled his fists.

Desmond lowered his head but kept eye contact, jaw clenched.

Declan looked past the man at Remi.

Then he yelled.

Guns came out and up from the man in the suit, Redhead and the woman. Declan stopped in his tracks.

Remi was lying across one of the cots, blood visible across the side of her face.

"She's not dead, not yet," the man said. "She got a little too mouthy so I showed her what that gets you in my house. I hit her a little too hard, I suppose. She fell right over like a twig in the wind."

Declan was absolutely seething. His chest was rising and falling in rage-fueled pants. He turned to the man in the suit.

"You said she was fine," he roared.

The man in the suit shared a look with the other. He didn't seem too happy, but he offered Declan no explanation or apology.

Then Declan was staring back at the man he was going to kill.

The triplets had tried their best to describe what their abductor looked like after they were rescued. Madi had talked about his eyes so dark they looked black and made you feel cold when they were on you. Brown hair like dry mud and messy like mud, too. Caleb had focused on his stature. He wasn't too tall but was wide. Strong but slow. Not overweight but not rail thin. Average. Desmond, on the other hand, had gotten more emotional with his descriptions.

One had always stuck with Declan.

"He was quiet but looked like he wanted to break us just because he could," eight-year-old Desmond had said. It was a statement that had held more weight than the others, considering that same man had badly broken his leg during the initial attack and then made him suffer with it for days.

Now, standing close enough to strangle him, Declan saw what young Desmond had seen.

The man wanted to break them. All of them.

And Declan was over it.

"What do you want?"

The man kept smiling.

"My name is William Gallagher," he started. "And I tell you that to remind you that you won't be leaving this cabin, so having my name does nothing for you. As for you, well, I'll never forget you." He looked past Declan's shoulder and listed the triplets off as he looked at them. "Desmond, Madeline and Caleb. It's been a while, hasn't it? I've been keeping tabs on you three. Late congratulations on your marriages and children. Your careers are also touching. Not what I would have picked had I had a choice, but it doesn't really matter in the end, does it?"

Declan had to breathe in slowly through his nose and

let out a breath through his mouth. It was the only way to keep from running at William.

He seemed to sense Declan's struggle with his rage.

"Dean wanted me to take you. Did you know that?" William said. "But if Dean wanted a distraction by taking one of Michael Nash's kids, boy howdy at the distraction taking three would be." His smile twisted upside down. Anger flashed across his expression. "I had everything planned out. But what I hadn't foreseen was how much heat taking you three would be. And after you escaped?" He shook his head, anger apparent on his face. "Dean decides not to pay me. Skips town. So what do I have to do? Go underground. Give up *my* life to hide as the entire country looks for my face. My scarred hand. *Me.* And all because I *gave a damn about you dying.*"

At this he looked at Desmond.

What was more famous than the abduction itself was how the triplets had escaped. After having his leg broken and untreated, by day three Desmond was in immense pain and in a bad way. Madi and Caleb knew that if they didn't get him help soon he could die. So, in a last-ditch effort, they'd decided to have him play dead.

Up until this point William had only ever brought them food. But when they started screaming and crying, saying that Desmond had stopped breathing, he'd run in to check. The moment he was trying to find a pulse was the moment everything changed.

It didn't matter who you asked, neither Madi, Caleb nor Desmond could remember exactly what happened next. The best they could describe it was that they'd simply synced up. Become a hive mind. They'd attacked William as one unit and gotten to the other side of the door to lock it. Together they'd run into the woods, bloody, broken and scarred.

When Caleb had brought the cops back to the cabin after they'd been found, William was gone.

"We couldn't have done it had you not broken my leg in the first place," Desmond shot back.

William let out a low, tense laugh.

"You don't understand the danger you're in, son. For years I missed out on the life I wanted, living in the shadows, waiting. So I decided to spend those years building something that could do what I'd been forced to do. All for the purpose of destroying everyone who forced me to abandon what I'd loved."

"You started the Fixers," Caleb said.

William nodded.

"And I used them to torment you all the last few years. Help those who despised you, who wanted to harm those you loved." He shared a look with the man in the suit. It wasn't a kind one. He didn't explain it, either. "You might have prevailed each time but you also were waiting. Waiting for the other shoe to drop." William extended his hands out wide. "Now it has."

"Why now?" Madi asked, voice sharp.

"I wanted you to build your lives. Make careers. Fall in love. Create families. I was getting restless waiting for our dear sheriff to find someone. But then his truck broke down and, well, the mouthy one behind me came into the picture. That was enough for me to start."

"So, Lydia, she's a Fixer." Declan said it because he

already believed it to be true. "She used Jonah to get to Remi."

William snorted.

"You want to know a fun thing about small towns? You get a happy coincidence once in a while. See, Lydia was brought in only to do whatever plan I saw fit. She was supposed to blend in first and build up some grace with the locals until I had that plan. And what better family to attach to than those who ran the Heartland Ranch? Childhood friends to the Nashes? It was a shock to us all when we realized that, not only were you and Miss Hudson no longer just friends, that she was pregnant with your child." His grin was sickening. "Having Lydia and the others try to take the mother of a future Nash child, even though it didn't work out the way I wanted? Well that was almost as fun as planting a note in a wall, knowing that just the mention of it would drive you mad. Watching you Nashes obsess has become a fun pastime of mine throughout the years. I think, when this is over, that's what I'll miss most."

William took a small step forward. Not close enough that Declan could lunge at him but close enough that Declan's muscles started tensing up, ready for anything. His mirth was gone. He had gotten to what he really wanted to say. "I want you all to know that your violent deaths will become a horror story every man, woman and child will know. A nighttime terror that will haunt your families, your loved ones, your friends, your co-workers. Strangers. I had to live in the shadows and you'll never leave the spotlight. Not even in death."

He turned to the man in the suit. He nodded, but neither man made a move. William looked at Declan as he added one last thing.

"Any last words before *all* of you meet horrible ends?"

Declan took a quick breath.

Then he turned to the man in the suit and made sure his words were absolutely sincere.

This was it.

"I want to hire you."

The man in the suit raised his eyebrow. Redhead and the woman laughed. So did William. The man didn't.

"Come again?"

Declan turned to face him completely, angling away from William. So did Madi, Caleb and Desmond.

"My father was a good man," he started. "But when he couldn't find who was behind the abduction, he became obsessed. Every day, every night. Weekends. He worked the case until it was all he did. Holidays, birthdays. He started to hate every special day that families are supposed to enjoy together. They were reminders that the years were going by and he was no closer to figuring it out. He pushed my mother away first, and then, when we all started to move on, he dug in so deep that he sacrificed himself to it. The obsession. Then he died, and even though I knew not to become him because I'd seen what it did, I still followed his example." Declan motioned to the room around him. "I own this place. This hell pit. Because *he* did and he willed it to me. No explanation. No note. Just a deed and an unspoken direction." That was something no one in his family knew. He could feel six baby blue eyes look in his direction. He kept on. "And I went into law enforcement and I started to obsess. I started walking that line between doing what I wanted and doing what he wanted."

Declan glanced at William. He still looked smug.

"When William took the kids, he ended whatever chance we had at a normal life. That includes you." This part was a gamble, but it was a theory they had kicked around before coming to Well Water.

Declan motioned to his hand. To the scar that matched William's.

"You were right earlier. I don't know much about you, but I *do* know you follow contracts. You never betray them. *That's* your code. And since William is your father, I'm going to assume he doesn't have a contract, does he?"

A pin could have dropped and they would have heard it.

The man in the suit didn't dispute a word he'd said.

Which meant they had been right. The man in the suit wasn't the boss, he was their abductor's son.

"You want to hire me to kill my father?" he asked after a moment.

Declan shook his head.

"I want to hire you and the Fixers to get Remi, take her to the hospital and tell them she's pregnant, and then do what you all do best. Disappear." Declan looked around the room to the suits ready to mock such an outrageous idea. He pointed to William, who was looking less smug. "At his prime he was bested by three eight-year-olds. Then he spent most of his life plotting against them when he could have easily killed us time and time again. You've been around here. You know who we are. We're fathers and mothers and husbands and wives. We're law enforcement. We're charitable and charming and kind. This town loves us. If you kill us? All because an old man's pissed he messed up a job by not following orders in the first place? You'll be hunted to the ground by our loved ones. And if they don't find you, they'll have kids that will grow up and hunt your kids down. The cycle will never end."

Declan went back to the man in the suit.

"Let's show our fathers we're stronger than they ever were."

William made a noise. A snort that clearly said he thought Declan was crazy.

But he wasn't paying attention to the suits. Their expressions had turned thoughtful and their gazes had turned to the man in the suit.

He considered Declan. He considered his father. Then he looked at the scar on his hand.

That was when Declan knew.

"There's money in the trunk of the car, where the spare tire is. I don't know your going rate, but it should be enough."

The man turned back to him. He nodded.

"Your contract has been accepted."

"What!" William was livid. His son paid him no mind.

"We'll take Miss Hudson to the hospital and let them know she's pregnant. Then you won't ever see us again." He nodded to Redhead and the woman. They went to Remi and scooped her up. Declan wished it could be him, but the Nash siblings had already guessed that while the man in the suit might accept their contract, he wouldn't go so far as to interfere with his dad.

The other suits seemed to agree and, just like that, the man in the suit became the real boss of the Fixers. He saw to Remi being taken to the stairs and only stopped at the door. He turned around and looked his father up and down. His last words before he left the room, however, were for them all.

"There's a gun in the middle kitchen drawer. Good luck."

The door shut and the sound of it locking became the background noise to a whirl of motion.

William was faster than Declan would ever give him credit for. He couldn't grab him in time. None of them could though they tried.

Madi got to him just as he flung the drawer open. She grabbed at his face, lashing out with her nails. It tore at his skin, making him yell so loud it hurt Declan's ears. Still he pulled the gun out and turned. Desmond gave his own battle cry as he hit the man in the gut with a devastating tackle. He, Madi and William slammed backward into the wall. The gun hit the ground and skidded away but William kept struggling.

Caleb joined the fray next with a punch that hit William's face so hard it echoed.

Declan scooped up the gun. He aimed it at William but there was no reason to use it. William had gone slack from the hit even though Madi held one arm, Desmond held the other, and Caleb had his hands against his chest so he wouldn't move an inch from where he was.

Despite everything, Declan smiled.

The Nash triplets had, once again, bested their abductor.

He wasn't dead but, this time, there wasn't a chance in hell that he was getting away.

Chapter Twenty-Two

Remi was shocked.

By many, many things.

First, she was shocked to wake up in her car being driven by the man in the suit. They were alone, which made her feel such an intense wave of anger and anguish that she nearly got sick again. The throbbing headache from being knocked out by his boss in the basement wasn't helping.

"Declan hired me to take you to the hospital," he'd said when she moved. "From there you can call for help to go out to the cabin. It'll only be the Nash family and one other man."

Remi hadn't known what to say or believe but, sure enough, he'd dropped her off right outside the hospital doors. Then he'd gotten out of her car, which apparently Declan had driven to the cabin, and stepped into one that had been following them.

And then he'd left.

The second shock was, after sending almost every member in law enforcement to Well Water Cabin, she got a call from Declan. Remi blamed the pregnancy hormones on how hard she cried at hearing his voice.

The shocks only got better after that.

Remi was seen by a doctor alongside her mother, who had finally made it to the hospital. Together they learned something that made them both freak out and squeal at the same time. After that Remi found out her father was awake and asking for her.

She hugged him fiercely, told him what she'd just found out and then the decisions she'd come to while being trapped in the basement. She'd cried again as he'd teared up. Josh and Jonah were next on the list for some familial love and the good news.

Then Declan arrived as she settled into a seat in the lobby to wait for him.

He ran in, saw her and was upon her before she could stand. He only broke their kiss to ask a volley of questions.

"Are you okay? Why are you out here? How's the baby?"

Remi laughed.

"I have a headache but am okay. I came out here to wait for you." Remi took a deep breath, then let it out. "And the babies are fine."

Declan's eyes tripled in size.

He smiled like a wild man.

"Babies?"

Remi held up her fingers.

"It's still too early to really tell anyone but, there are two sacs, Declan. *Two.*"

She laughed, unable to stop the giddiness.

Declan shook his head, then was laughing.

"I'm guessing that means you're okay with the idea of having twins?"

"Are kidding me? I'd love it!" He laughed again, throwing his head back. Then he wrapped his arms around her. "Man, my family is going to flip. The singleton Nash might have twins?"

He pulled away from her and dipped low for another kiss.

Then those green eyes she loved were on her. Suddenly his expression changed to a serious one.

"Huds, we said we were going to have a talk about the future and here's what I'm thinking. I want to move to Colorado with you," he said. "I want to raise our kids together, in the same place. I want to wake up next to you and go to sleep with you in my arms."

That was the second biggest shock of the night.

"You'd give up being sheriff? You'd leave your family?"

Declan put his hand on her stomach. Remi could have melted.

"You're my family, too. And I'd cross oceans for you if that's what you wanted."

Butterflies dislodged and had a frenzy in her stomach.

"Well, look at that. My wild cowboy ready to hang up his hat for me." She ran a hand across his cheek. Every part of her softened. "I suppose this is a good time to tell you my new life plan. I have a feeling you're going to really like it."

ONE CHRISTMAS PASSED.

And then another.

By the third Christmas, so much had changed.

And so much hadn't.

Declan sat on his horse wearing his cowboy hat. Desmond and Caleb wore theirs while Madi was sitting on the fence next to the stable wearing her boots. She was pregnant again and her bump was the reason she'd decided to sit on the fence rather than a horse. Still, she wanted to hang around her siblings until Julian showed up so they could go home.

"You know, Ma is bringing a date to Christmas Eve dinner, right?" she asked, no hard feelings in the words. Between Desmond and Riley becoming parents, Caleb and Nina expanding the retreat, and Madi and Julian preparing for their fourth child, spending time together had lessened. They still had Sunday dinners together, but that was at their mother's, which meant gossiping about her hadn't been ideal.

"It's about time," Desmond said with a smile. Caleb mirrored it.

"Y'all do know she's been seeing Christian in secret for over a year, right?"

Declan laughed.

"Yeah, it's not like you can keep a secret in this town. I'm glad she's making it public, though. Now we don't have to pretend like we have no idea why he keeps showing up around the ranch even though he lives in Kilwin."

Madi laughed and bounced her foot in the air. She rubbed her belly.

"I think Dad would approve, despite him and Christian's differences from back in the day."

They all agreed. During what felt like a lifetime ago, their father had believed Christian was connected to the triplets' abduction. It had put a wall of resentment and discord between the men and the Nash family. That was until Christian had proven he was a great man after helping Madi survive the family's first brush with the Fixers. Since then he'd become friends with the family. More so with their mother. Dorothy Nash had been nothing but happy the last year or so and they knew it wasn't all because they'd put William Gallagher behind bars for good. Though, having him locked up had definitely helped.

For a man who had spent years cultivating a group who would rather die than spill their secrets, William became a very talkative man once in handcuffs. He said he did so to take Dean Lawson down with him, detailing their arrangement and what had really happened all those years ago. Lawson, who had passed away at the bar that night, lost the reputation he'd built for years, as well. And that had been William's goal.

He was big on trying to hurt people, even after death.

As for his son, the man in the suit, he mostly stayed true to his word. A month after everything had settled down, he visited Declan outside of the grocery store of all places.

"I don't think you understand what 'I won't see you ever again' means," Declan had greeted. The man in the suit had smirked.

"Don't worry, this is a quick social visit."

Declan knew the man wasn't good, but he couldn't bring himself to be wary of him, either. Especially since the Fixers had been rumored to have disappeared from, not only Overlook, but all of Wildman County.

"For what it's worth, I'm sorry about your dad," Declan had found himself saying. He'd later blame the kindness on the fact that the man had taken Remi to the hospital and, honestly, had saved all of their lives by taking the contract in the first place.

"For what it's worth, I'm sorry about yours, too."

They'd shared a small companionable silence. One of understanding. Then they were back to their normal roles.

"You know, this is the only time I'll let you go free," Declan had said. "So after you leave my sight, you better stay out of it."

The man in the suit had laughed.

"Remember how we agreed that you don't know me?" he'd asked. "Well, let me enlighten you on something. While my dad was amassing money to help with your destruction, I was stealing and saving it. The second I'm out of your sight I'll be heading to a private airfield and on my way to a beautiful, remote beach somewhere very tropical. And *then* I'll disappear."

"Still, very brazen of you to show back up here again."

The man in the suit started to walk toward a car near them.

"I can afford to be brazen, Sheriff. I bet you still haven't found *any* record of my existence, have you?" He'd said it with a smile and he'd been right. No one had been able to find any hint that he existed, not even his name. "Don't feel bad. While my father spent decades waiting to reveal himself when the right time came, I spent the same time waiting to disappear."

The man in the suit had pointed to Declan's truck.

"Consider that an early baby shower gift," he'd said. "For what it's worth, I don't hate that you Nashes might now have a shot at a happy ending. And consider this the only time I'll ever break a contract."

He'd already been gone by the time Declan saw what he'd left in Fiona's front seat.

It was the bag of money he and his siblings had collected to pay for their contract with the Fixers back at Well Water. On top of the bag were two ribbons. One pink, one blue.

Declan and Remi had received another gift after they'd married that he believed to be from the man. It was a postcard of an island with well wishes and an exorbitant amount of money that they'd decided to give to charity. The card had been signed "the Whisperer."

Other than that, Declan hadn't seen or heard of the man in the suit or the Fixers since.

"I think Dad would have liked this, too," Caleb said, bringing Declan back to the present. He motioned to the four of them. "Us, I mean, but, especially you."

Declan was surprised to see those three sets of baby blues turn to him. Caleb continued.

"We realized this morning when we were helping set up the Christmas lights that we somehow have been idiots and haven't told you this outright and in clear words. So, get ready for the mushiness."

They all shared a look.

Desmond spoke next.

"Thank you, Declan."

He didn't understand.

"For what?"

Madi's smile was small but true.

"For giving us peace."

It was such a simple statement but it did something Declan hadn't thought possible. A weight had been lifted. The guilt, the heartache... It all blew away in the nice December breeze.

Movement caught his eye at the edge of the field.

"You guys are going to make me cry in front of my wife," he said with a genuine smile.

Madi laughed.

"Like you didn't blubber when Michael and Lysa were born," she teased.

"And don't forget that tearing up you did at the wedding," Caleb added with a grin.

Declan laughed and didn't deny either accusation. Other than his kids being born, his wedding to Remi had been one of the best days of his life.

It had been a small, perfect ceremony held in the no-man's-land between the Nash Family Ranch and Hudson Heartland. To show they approved of Declan, Gale Hudson had officiated while Josh and Jonah had walked Remi down the aisle of flowers and grass. Her mother and stepfather had held the twins while his mother and Christian had distracted the rest of the grandchildren. Every Nash sibling and spouse were either groomsmen or bridesmaids.

"Don't act like you didn't drop a tear or two," Desmond said to Caleb.

Caleb in turn swatted at him, which riled Desmond up. Soon they were racing around the barn and up toward Caleb's house. A car started up the drive and Madi waved Declan off.

"That's Julian," she said. "You can go on to your wife now, Sheriff."

"If I could, I'd swoop down and kiss you on the cheek, little sister," he said, half-mocking. She laughed.

"And if I wasn't the size of a beach ball I'd stand up and accept it."

Declan laughed and soon he was off riding. He slowed as Remi did, meeting him in the middle.

She was as beautiful as a sunset and he told her as much.

"You keep sweet-talking me like that, Mr. Nash, and we might be catching up to Madi and Julian's kid count tonight."

Declan chuckled.

"We did say we'd start sometime after the kids were walking," he pointed out. "Though now I can't see where the sense in that is."

"We're attracted to adventure, I suppose. Why else would we be building a house with a set of twins and two stressful jobs?"

Declan ticked the reasons off on his fingers as he listed them.

"Because my house was too small. We're sentimental fools who thought it would be nice to live on the same stretch of land we got married on. We didn't plan to get pregnant with twins, though I'm over the moon it happened. *And* because we actually love our jobs."

Remi, who was now chief financial officer at Desmond's foundation, nodded at each point.

"Don't you come at me with answers that make sense."

"Oh, I'll come at you with something all right, cowgirl."

He winked at her, which made Remi throw her head back as she laughed again.

Then she was all smiles.

"Only if you can catch me, cowboy."

Remi was off on her horse, pointed toward their home, faster than Declan could whistle.

Before he followed after her, Declan turned around and looked at his family and the ranch he'd been born on and would probably spend the rest of his days around.

Caleb, Desmond and Madi were still hanging around, laughing, talking and riding. His mother was up at the house, not five minutes away, singing Christmas carols and baking gingerbread cookies, he had no doubt.

Declan had spent years worrying about his family. Worrying that they'd never be whole again. That they'd never *truly* find happiness. That life wasn't as kind as it was mean.

Yet, sitting astride his horse in a field he used to ride with his father, Declan Nash *really* did feel it, too.

Peace.

* * * * *

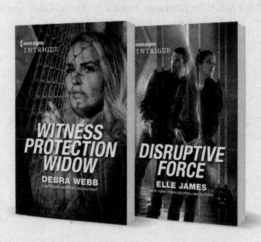

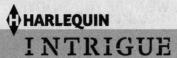

He had a lead.

The partial fingerprint he'd lifted from the murder
scene hadn't been a partial at all, but evidence of a severe
burn on the owner's index finger that altered the print.
He hadn't been able to get an ID with so few markers to
compare before leaving New York City a year ago. But
now, Blackhawk Security forensic expert Vincent Kalani
finally had a chance to bring down a killer.

He hauled his duffel bag higher on his shoulder. He
had to get back to New York, convince his former
commanding officer to reopen the case. His muscles
burned under the weight as he ducked beneath the small
passenger plane's wing and climbed inside. Cold Alaskan
air drove beneath his heavy coat, but catching sight of the
second passenger already aboard chased back the chill.

HIEXP0920

"Shea Ramsey." Long, curly dark hair slid over her shoulder as jade-green eyes widened in surprise. His entire body nearly gave in to the increased sense of gravity pulling at him had it not been for the paralysis working through his muscles. Officer Shea Ramsey had assisted Blackhawk Security with investigations in the past at the insistence of Anchorage's chief of police, but her form-fitting pair of jeans, T-shirt and zip-up hoodie announced she wasn't here on business. Hell, she was a damn beautiful woman, an even better investigator and apparently headed to New York. Same as him. "Anchorage Police Department's finest, indeed."

"What the hell are you doing here?" Shea shuffled her small backpack at her feet, crossing her arms over her midsection. The tendons between her shoulders and neck corded with tension as she stared out her side of the plane. No mistaking the bitterness in her voice. "Is Blackhawk following me now?"

"Should we be?"

Don't miss
The Line of Duty *by Nichole Severn,*
available October 2020 wherever
Harlequin Intrigue books and ebooks are sold.

Harlequin.com